IMPERIAL
SPLENDOUR

Barbara Cartland

IMPERIAL
SPLENDOUR

E. P. Dutton
New York

For information contact: E. P. Dutton, 2 Park Avenue
New York, N.Y. 10016

Library of Congress Cataloging in Publication Data

Cartland, Barbara, 1902-
Imperial splendour.
I. Title.
PZ3.C247Im 1979 [PR6005.A765] 823'.9'12 78-31315
ISBN: 0-525-13198-1
Published simultaneously in Canada by Clarke, Irwin
& Company Limited, Toronto and Vancouver

10 9 8 7 6 5 4 3 2 1
First Edition

This book is dedicated to the Earl Mountbatten of Burma, who first suggested I should visit Russia to obtain the background for this novel. He also helped me with many of the authentic details.

AUTHOR'S NOTE

As Napoleon waited in Moscow for an Armistice, the vascillating Tsar Alexander was transformed into a man fortified by a deep religious fervour. He replied that he could not negotiate while "one enemy soldier remains on Russian soil."

After five weeks Napoleon had no option but to withdraw his Army and begin the long trek home. But he had left it too late.

On November 4 the snow began to fall and two days later the temperature was many degrees below freezing. Lack of food and clothing, and the savagery of the Russian peasants, resulted in the roads being strewn with dead men, guns, and horses. Nearly half-a-million of the *Grande Armée* failed to reach France.

In April 1814 Napoleon abdicated and was exiled to the island of Elba. When Alexander entered Paris, the crowds went wild, and his own country begged him to accept the title of "Alexander the Blessed." It was the Tsar who, at the Congress of Vienna, first had the idea of a League of Nations.

The Russians rebuilt Moscow, and when I visited Leningrad in 1978 I saw how brilliantly they had re-built that city after the terrible devastation left by the Germans in 1941. The Palaces which had been looted, shelled, and blown up by mines are now elaborate, splendid, and exactly as when they were designed on the order of Catherine the Great.

The famous Duke of Wellington in 1826 thought St. Petersburg "the most beautiful town on earth."

Armand-Emmanuel *Duc* de Richelieu (1766–1822) held the post of Governor-General of New Russia until 1815. After the war he was twice Prime Minister of France under Louis XVIII.

La Sylphide launched the whole Romantic period of the Ballet and was performed in Paris in March 1832, in London in July, and in St. Petersburg in September.

The costume attributed to "Lami," with its long bell-shaped skirt, became the accepted attire of Ballerinas of the period and is still worn. Because it is so familiar and I wanted my readers to know exactly how Zoia looked, I have anticipated its performance in St. Petersburg by twenty years.

IMPERIAL
SPLENDOUR

Chapter One
1812

The Duke of Welminster walked across the room to pull back the curtains from the window and stare out at the Neva.

The pale sunlight, which later would deepen to a red and heat the river, one of the shortest in the world, was shimmering on the water.

It reflected the brilliant shining gold on the needle-like spire of the Peter and Paul Cathedral on the farther shore, and the Duke could also see the bastions and battlements of the Fortress built by Peter the Great.

However, he was for the moment concerned not with the beauty of St. Petersburg, which had left him surprised by the perfection of its architecture, but with the Russian Army, awaiting their Commander-in-Chief's conclusion as to the direction in which the French intended to advance.

The Duke's contemplation was interrupted by a soft cry of protest.

"Have you forgotten me?" a woman's voice asked. "I am still here, and wanting you."

1

There was no mistaking the invitation and the seductive undertone which made the words, spoken in English but with a distinct trace of a Russian accent, sound passionately alluring.

The Duke turned, a smile on his lips.

There was no doubt that the Princess Katharina Bagration was very lovely, in fact one of the loveliest women he had ever seen.

Lying back against the lace-edged pillows, with her hair falling over her white shoulders, her huge eyes seeming to fill her whole face, she looked very much younger than she actually was.

There was an Oriental mystery about her, an Andalusian charm, and, when she was dressed, a Parisian elegance.

It was not surprising, the Duke thought, that Tsar Alexander I had chosen her to spy on him—a fact of which he had been aware the moment he had arrived in St. Petersburg.

The Duke was very experienced in the art of intrigue and had carried out a number of unofficial diplomatic missions with such success that he had in fact not been surprised when the Prime Minister, Lord Liverpool, had sent for him.

"I want your help, Welminster," he had said, "and I think you can guess where I wish you to go."

"To Russia?" the Duke had queried.

"Exactly!" the Prime Minister replied.

Lord Castlereagh, the Foreign Secretary, who was in the Cabinet-Room, interposed:

"For God's sake, Welminster, find out what is happening. The reports I receive contradict themselves to the point where I do not know whether I am on my head or my heels as far as that enigmatic country is concerned."

The irritation in the Foreign Secretary's voice was

very evident, and the Duke could understand his frustration.

Tsar Alexander had kept not only the British but most of Europe confused by his behaviour during the last few years.

Even Napoleon Bonaparte might be excused for finding him incomprehensible.

Having moved through the first years of his reign, at the beginning of the century, as a shadowy, indecisive figure, Alexander's attention had become focussed on Bonaparte.

The Corsican's astonishing Military successes had turned the whole of Europe into a turmoil.

The Tsar could not make up his mind whether to join a coalition against the French or to continue his father's policy of friendship.

Napoleon had actually suggested to Tsar Paul, Alexander's father, that France and Russia should partition the world, but when Bonaparte had trampled into the dust the terms of the Treaty of Amiens, the Russian Sovereign wrote that he seemed to be "one of the most infamous tyrants that history has produced."

After the disaster of Austerlitz, when the twenty-eight-year-old Tsar Alexander, leading his Army as Commander-in-Chief, had been completely routed, his gallantry had deserted him.

He had ridden away from the battle-field alone, dismounted, to collapse under an apple-tree, where he had wept convulsively.

Although he tried to excuse himself by blaming the Austrians, the Russians suffered another disastrous defeat at Friedland.

It was then, to the amazement of the Russian people, that Alexander had signed a "Treaty of Friendship" with the French in which he promised to take part in the Continental Blockade against England.

This had brought him extreme unpopularity with the Russian people, together with the fact that after Catherine the Great's victories they could not adjust themselves to a number of ignominious defeats.

The preceding year, 1811, Alexander had listened to his subjects and refused to send soldiers to fight for the French, and, what was more, had refused to close Russian ports to neutral shipping and uphold the blockade against England.

"I cannot help thinking," a famous British General had said to the Duke in London, "that if it comes to a showdown, Russia will prove a poor match for Napoleon's *Grande Armée.*"

The Duke had felt inclined to agree with him, but now that he was actually in Russia he began to have his doubts.

In fact, when yesterday the Tsar had shown him a letter from Count Rostopchin, the Governor of Moscow, he had found the contents very convincing.

The Govenor had written:

> *Your Empire, Sire, has two powerful defenders—vast space and its climate. The Emperor of all Russia will be formidable at Moscow, terrible at Karzan, and invincible at Tobolsk.*

"Stop thinking about war, Blake," the Princess Katharina now cried insistently. "I can find something far more interesting to talk about."

The Duke, standing by the bed, knew what such a conversation involved, but instead of surrendering to the invitation of her lips, he replied:

"I think it is time you returned to your own room."

"There is no hurry."

"I am thinking of your reputation."

The Princess laughed and it was a low, musical sound.

"You are the only man I know who is so considerate, or is it perhaps that I am boring you?"

There was no doubt that she assumed that this was an impossibility, and the Duke, with just a touch of cynicism in his voice, answered:

"How could I be so ungallant?"

"You are very handsome, *mon cher,*" the Princess said, "as far too many women have told you. I adore handsome men, and no man could be a more alluring lover."

She then broke into French, as if it was easier to express herself in that language when she spoke of love.

French was the language of the nobility in St. Petersburg and French culture was a status symbol. Someone had told the Duke on arrival:

"Everything is uneatable for dinner if it is not dressed by a French Chef, no gown is elegant if it is not a Parisian one, and yet there is no-one in the whole city who does not blaspheme against Bonaparte and lament Lord Nelson!"

"You are very beautiful, Katharina!" the Duke said now in French. "But I still think you should leave me for what is left of the night."

The Princess made a petulant little sound. Then, bending forward to reveal the exquisite curves of her naked breasts, she put her hand on the Duke's.

"You are too serious," she said. "Let us be happy and enjoy ourselves. After all, what is Russia to you?"

"An ally," the Duke replied, "if a somewhat vacillating one."

Katharina laughed softly, then said:

"Tell me what you want to know about your 'ally' and I will give you the right answers."

"I am sure of that," he replied. "I am only wondering what such information will cost me."

Katharina laughed again.

She was well aware that the Duke knew why she had sought him out; why she had flirted enticingly with him since he had arrived at the Winter Palace; and why last night after he had retired to bed a secret panel in the wall of his room had opened and she had appeared unexpectedly.

That in fact was not entirely true, because the Duke had been expecting her, although not in the particular manner by which she had effected her entrance.

"You know, of course," Lord Castlereagh had said to him in London, "that the Tsar employs the loveliest women in St. Petersburg to spy on our Ambassador and any other Emissary we send to Russia."

He had seen the smile on the Duke's face and added:

"Not that that, Welminster, will be a novelty for you."

"I will admit it is something which has happened in the past," the Duke replied, "and, having heard of the beauty of the women at the Court of St. Petersburg, I am quite looking forward to the experience."

"Careful!" the Foreign Secretary warned.

"Of what?" the Duke enquired. "Giving away State secrets, most of which I suspect are known to the Russians already, or of losing my heart?"

"The latter is something which had not entered into my calculations," Lord Castlereagh replied with a touch of irony.

The Duke had been expecting an enchantress, but he had to give the Tsar full marks for his choice of the Princess.

As it happened, the Duke already knew a great deal about Katharina Bagration. She was half-

Russian, half-Polish, and had married at twenty a General years older than herself.

A Countess in her own right, with Royal blood in her veins, with her husband she was admitted to the highest circles of the Russian Court.

The fact that she was highly intelligent as well as beautiful, together with the traces in her of a Mongolian ancestry, gave her the faint air of Oriental mystery which made her unique even amongst a host of other beautiful women.

It was the Tsar who had ordered his Foreign Minister to use this effervescent and lovely young woman as a spy.

The Duke had heard what had happened at Katharina's first assignment.

She had been told to make the acquaintance of Count Metternich, the Austrian Delegate to Dresden, who the Russian Diplomats in Vienna insisted was of far greater importance than his youth and minor appointment suggested.

Count Metternich, then an almost unknown young man, was described on the secret files in the Kremlin as an intimate of the Emperor of Austria and the instrument who had been primarily responsible for the downfall of Thugut.

Princess Katharina, young, lovely, but with a shrewd little mind hidden behind her child-like face, had called at the Legation in Dresden, and as footmen opened the door, it happened that Count Metternich was passing through the Hall.

He waited, expecting one of the Imperial Couriers with grave news.

Then he saw a small, exquisite figure framed in the sunlight against the dark Hallway.

She was wearing one of the thin, almost transparent muslin gowns that were the fashion, and against the sun her body showed through the diaphanous material like a beautiful marble statue.

Count Metternich was for the moment spellbound into a strange stillness.

He said afterwards to one of his friends, who repeated it to the Duke:

"She was like a beautiful, naked angel."

At that moment the young Austrian and the Russian Secret Agent fell in love.

Their affair was a wild, fiery, insatiable union of all-consuming passion which had all Dresden talking.

The Duke had trained himself to file away information about people, especially those involved in the Diplomatic World, and as soon as he was introduced to Princess Katharina in the Winter Palace he remembered that he had been told that within three months of her meeting with Count Metternich, she had found that she was to have a child.

It had been whispered about, argued over, discussed and re-discussed, and there was actually a great deal of speculation as to what would happen.

In fact, the Duke recalled, there had been an urgent command from the Tsar, who wished to safeguard his beautiful Agent's reputation at all costs.

General Bagration went through the ritual of announcing that his marriage was shortly to be blessed with a child, and after the birth of a daughter he formally acknowledged paternity.

The Tsar was no less accommodating and the Court of St. Petersburg recorded the birth.

The baby was in fact handed over to Count Metternich's adoring, patient, and very understanding wife.

Utterly without conscience about the love-children he fathered, he was only grateful that his love-affair could continue and that whatever was said privately, there would be no outward scandal.

Ten years later the Duke, however, was quite certain that because Katharina had been so successful with by now the most outstanding Diplomat in Europe, the Tsar had chosen her to win another triumph, where he himself was concerned.

He was sure that the efficiency of the Russian Secret Service had noted that he was extremely fastidious where women were concerned, that he was the most sought-after bachelor in England, and that if they had recorded his many love-affairs they would doubtless by this time have filled many files in the Diplomatic Archives.

At the same time, he found Katharina's expertise and her sophisticated art in love-making a very pleasant part of his visit.

The Duke was quite ruthless where his interests were concerned.

If he had been approached by a woman who did not attract him or by one who offended his very fastidious taste when making love, he would have had no compunction about locking his door or, if that proved ineffective, turning her from his bed.

But Katharina had appealed to him sensually, and her body was, as many other men had found, irresistible.

The Duke had thought, as the passion they felt for each other burst into flame in the huge carved and gilded bed in a room decorated in the French manner and filled with priceless pictures that Catherine the Great's Agents had acquired from France, that she was the complement to everything that proclaimed culture.

When she had captured Count Metternich's heart

she had been very young and perhaps he had been her first lover after her marriage.

But now, the Duke thought, she had blossomed into a woman, polished like a flawless gem into a brilliance that aroused the admiration of the mind as well as the desires of the body.

The Duke enjoyed the duel they exchanged with words, witty and provocative, even while she used every feminine wile to enslave him physically.

Now as he looked at her with his grey eyes, she leant back against the pillows and with her long-fingered little hands pulled the sheet over her nakedness until it was just beneath her chin.

There was something young and modest in the movement, and yet at the same time it was a deliberately seductive action, thought out, perhaps practised, like the ritual steps of a Ballerina, and the Duke appreciated the very artistry of it.

"What do you think about, Katharina," he asked, "when you are not 'working'?"

For a moment she looked at him doubtfully, then made no pretence not to understand the innuendo that lay behind his words.

"Now I am thinking of you," she said softly, "and there is no reason to think of myself."

It was an answer, he thought, that revealed the very subtlety of her mind.

Who else would she think about, when she was not acting on the Tsar's instructions, but herself, her fiery, passionate Russian nature making it an absorbing subject.

The Duke glanced towards the elaborate gold and diamond encrusted clock which stood on the marble mantelpiece.

It was one of hundreds of beautiful clocks which decorated the great apartments of the Winter Palace

which on three floors extended for half-a-mile, and had been part of Peter the Great's collection.

"It is five o'clock," he said, "and in four hours I have promised to breakfast with the Tsar. Until then I intend to sleep, Katharina."

There was a note in his voice which told her it would be useless to plead with him.

She merely smiled, and, rising from the bed apparently completely unselfconscious of her nakedness, walked to the chair on which she had thrown down the elaborate satin and lace negligé in which she had entered the room.

She might have had a child, but her body was still that of a beautiful naked angel, as Klements Metternich had described her.

Wrapped in her negligé, she slipped her small feet into a pair of velvet mules embroidered with pearls.

"Sleep well, my adorable Englishman!" she said. "I shall count the hours until I can kiss you again."

She flashed him a smile which gave her face a sudden witchery, then moved across the room.

She touched the panel in the wall. It opened, and without looking back she stepped into the dark aperture. Then the panel swung back and closed behind her.

The Duke sat still for a moment, then got into bed and closed his eyes, but he found that for the moment the sleep he desired eluded him.

His brain was still active and again he was thinking not of Katharina and the fire they had ignited in each other, but of Russia and of the *Grande Armée* of France, 600,000 strong and immensely impressive.

At the same time, the Duke argued with himself that a third of the soldiers were unwilling German conscripts drawn from subject territories.

The first thing he had learnt on reaching St. Peters-

burg was that Alexander had been astounded when he had heard that Napoleon was heading towards the ancient and sacred Capital of Russia.

He had never imagined that the Emperor would actually attempt to march to Moscow, and the thought of the inevitable carnage appalled him.

The one blessing from the Russian point of view, the Duke told himself, was the fact that the Tsar was not himself leading the Russian Armies.

His record as a Military Leader had been so disastrous that even now every set-back was attributed to his influence.

Because his sister had been so desperate she had written to him bluntly in a manner no-one else would have dared to do:

> *For God's sake do not decide to assume command yourself. There is no time to lose to give the Armies a Chief in whom the men will have confidence. As for you, you cannot inspire them with any.*

Amazingly, Alexander had heeded her pleas and left the Army.

He had travelled back to Moscow, then to St. Petersburg. Everywhere he heard criticisms of the High Command, and everywhere there was a cry for Kutuzov, whose name spelt magic for the people.

Alexander had no faith in General Kutuzov. He felt he was a figure from another century, but he decided to bow to popular demand, and told the Duke on his arrival:

"The public want him! I have appointed him! As for me—I wash my hands of the whole affair!"

The Duke understood that he was feeling peeved at being more or less deposed in favour of a sixty-

seven-year-old General who was lazy, licentious, and knew nothing of modern warfare.

Other people in the Palace, however, informed the Duke that Kutuzov, despite all his shortcomings, had the common sense born of long years of experience.

"He is slow but tenacious," an elderly statesman said, "lazy, but discerning, impassive but cunning!"

All this information the Duke conveyed in code by Special Courier to London.

He hoped with one of his mocking smiles that the Prime Minister and the Foreign Secretary would be able to make something out of it.

"The one thing about Russia," he told himself, "is that the unexpected always happens, and at least there is nothing monotonous here in the day-to-day life."

He realised that he was enjoying himself in his own rather cynical fashion, and with that thought in his mind he fell asleep.

* * *

At nine o'clock the Duke was admitted to the Tsar's private apartments.

To get there he walked through what seemed to him to be miles of the most beautiful and finely decorated rooms he had ever seen in his whole life.

He had been quite prepared for magnificence, for the stories of St. Petersburg's treasures and the splendour of its buildings had been told and retold in London.

It was the extravagant Empress Elizabeth who had pulled down the original wooden Winter Palace built by Peter the Great, and her architect Rastrelli in eight years covered an area of 2 million square feet with 1,050 rooms and 117 staircases.

The Empress Catherine when she came to power commissioned a Summer Palace that would outshine

Versailles, and in St. Petersburg she had added to the immense Winter Palace three buildings which were known as The Hermitage.

Between the buildings there were courtyards, heated in winter, where rare birds flitted amongst the trees and shrubberies.

The Empress had instructed her Ambassadors in Paris, Rome, and London to keep a sharp look-out for art bargains and they bought her many fine pictures by great masters such as Rembrandt, Tiepolo, Van Dyke, and Poussin.

The Duke glanced only perfunctorily at these magnificent works of art, for his mind was still concerned with Bonaparte's advance into Russia.

"It would be a tragedy," he told himself, "if treasures such as I see here should be lost to posterity."

When he reached the Tsar's apartments he was saluted by the sentries of the Grenadiers of Golden Guard.

Picked for their great height, out of all the regiments who effected their Russian bearskin they were the most gorgeous.

They wore white trousers and leggings, a black tunic with gold cuffs and collar, and cut-away tails— gold edged with red—upon which was fastened a cartridge-case embossed with a double-headed eagle.

The Duke found the Tsar waiting for him. Tall, fair-haired, and extremely handsome, it was easy to understand that the Russian people had looked at Alexander on his accession like a fairy-tale King come to save them from all their miseries.

Yet, when at twenty-four years of age he had ridden to his Coronation in 1801, a wit in St. James's had remarked:

"He was preceded by men who had murdered his grandfather, escorted by men who had murdered his father, and followed by men who would not think twice about murdering him!"

The Duke had heard from one of the Tsar's closest friends that when Alexander learnt of his father's cruel death he had burst into tears.

"I have not the strength to reign," he had said, sobbing to his wife. "Let someone else take my place."

The Duke had begun to think that the vision of Paul's strangled, battered body haunted the Tsar.

He was perceptive enough to know that Russians could suffer in their souls in a way that perhaps men of other nations were unable to do.

He had personally known the Tsar for some years and he was aware that he was often mentally convulsed with an inner agony which would, he thought, get worse rather than better as he grew older.

As he might have expected, this morning the Tsar was looking worried and speaking in a manner that had a touch of hysteria about it.

"The news is bad—very bad!" he told the Duke after he had greeted him.

"What have you learnt, Sire?" the Duke enquired.

"That Bonaparte is still marching towards Moscow!"

The Tsar spoke as if he could hardly bear to say the words, and then he sighed.

"God knows if it is the truth. To be honest, no-one seems to know that is happening."

The Duke was not astonished at this statement.

Methods of communication between the Army and the Tsar were haphazard and incompetent, as were a great many other things in Russia.

They sat down to breakfast, at which, as was usual, there were three kinds of bread.

One was a roll of white bread called *Kalatch,* as light as a feather and eaten hot, which was made from water brought especially from the river Moskva.

This water was delivered to all the Palaces in St. Petersburg, a custom which dated from the preceding century.

As they ate, the Tsar, instead of talking of what was happening to the troops under Kutuzov's direction, did nothing but quote passages from the Bible.

When the Duke looked at him in surprise, he explained:

"Yesterday I was told that my life-long friend Prince Alexander Golitzin is a traitor."

"That is impossible!" exclaimed the Duke, who knew the Prince.

"I tried not to believe what I was told," the Tsar said in a low voice, "but my informant said that he is constructing an impressive new Palace in which he could entertain Napoleon."

"Surely you do not believe such a wild tale?" the Duke asked.

"I went at once to visit Golitzin and asked him point-blank why he had chosen to build in such troubled times."

"What was his reply?" the Duke asked.

"The Prince answered: 'Your Imperial Majesty need not fear an invasion if you trust in Divine Providence.' "

The Duke raised his eye-brows but made no comment, and the Tsar went on:

"Golitzin then reached up to a bookshelf to take down a heavy volume of the Bible. It slipped to the floor and fell open at the page on which is printed Psalm Forty-one."

The Tsar paused impressively and the Duke said:

"I am afraid, Sire, I have forgotten that particular Psalm."

" 'I will say of the Lord: He is my refuge and

fortress: my God; in Him will I trust,' " the Tsar quoted.

His voice deepened and sounded impressive as he added:

"Golitzin convinced me that the opening of the Bible at that place was not a coincidence but a direct message from God."

"I hope the Prince was right," the Duke said drily.

"I am sure of it!" the Tsar said. "All night I have been reading the Bible and meditating on God and our situation. I believe we will be saved."

The Duke found it difficult not to remark that the Russians would certainly need the help of the Almighty because they could not hope to rely entirely on their Army.

Before he left England he had seen a report by Dr. Clarke, an Englishman who had visited the Tula arms factory two years earlier, in 1810, and had been appalled by the incompetence he found there.

His report said;

The machinery is ill-constructed and worse preserved. Everything seemed out-of-order. Workmen with long beards stood staring at each other, wondering what was to be done next, while their intendants or directors were drunk or asleep. Notwithstanding all this, they pretended to issue from the manufactory thirteen hundred muskets a week.

"What was the actual figure?" the Duke had asked.

"I have no idea," was the answer, "but we have learnt that the Russian muskets, besides being clumsily heavy, misfire five times out of ten and are liable to burst when they are discharged."

The Duke had thought that French spies must have

provided Napoleon Bonaparte with the same type of report as Dr. Clarke's.

He was doubtless anticipating that the resistance he would encounter on invading Russia would not be very effective against his own forces, which were highly organised and armed with the latest, most up-to-date equipment.

It would, however, have been pointless and merely unkind to repeat any of this to the Tsar. So the Duke did his best to talk of other things, knowing that there was nothing to be gained by having "The Little Father" of such a great country in the depths of despair.

'Perhaps things will turn out better than I anticipate,' he thought optimistically.

But when he moved amongst the Royal Family and other people staying in the Winter Palace, he found that they were as apprehensive as he was.

In fact, he found the whole atmosphere so depressing that he decided to call on Princess Ysevolsov, whom he had known for many years.

When he had arrived at the Palace he had found a letter, written in her usual animated and flowery manner, begging him to take the first opportunity of renewing their friendship.

She had written:

My poor Husband is of course away on the Battlefield, but I will receive You with open arms as one of my Closest and Dearest Friends in England, and I want too for You to meet my little Tania. She was only ten or eleven when You last saw her. Now She is very Beautiful, and when this tiresome War is over I want to present Her to our Friends in London and have Her make Her curtsey to the Queen at Buckingham Palace.

The Duke had read the letter and found quite a lot of information written "between the lines."

He knew that Prince Ysevolsov was one of the richest men in Russia. His family, like other members of the nobility for some generations past, not only owned huge estates but a fantastic number of serfs.

Prince Ysevolsov, the Duke remembered, was supposed to own over twenty-five thousand serfs in different provinces of the country.

He used them not only as goldsmiths, carpenters, and ebony-carvers, but for his private Theatrical Company and *Corps de Ballet*. He also had his own Theatre, where he gave performances for his friends.

The Prince's wife was as beautiful and valuable as were his other possessions.

She had, however, both Austrian and English blood in her, and she had often said to the Duke that she hoped her children when they grew up would not marry Russians.

The Duke, with his retentive memory, had now a very good idea why she was pressing upon him the attractions of her daughter Tania.

It would in fact be a very suitable match for the daughter of one of the richest and most important noblemen in Russia to marry one of the richest and most important noblemen of England.

But the Duke told himself that the Princess would be disappointed. He was now thirty-three and had so far evaded matrimony. Although from time to time he had come perilously near to being swept up the aisle, he had always at the last moment extracted himself from the difficult position.

In the past few years he had ensured that the danger did not occur, by having little or nothing to do with young girls.

His love-affairs were always conducted with mar-

ried women or widows and he made it clear from the
very beginning of his acquaintances with the latter
that he preferred his bachelor's freedom.

"You will have to marry one day in order to have
a son."

It was a sentence that was repeated and re-repeated
to him until he told himself that as far as he was
concerned, the Dukedom could go to his younger
brother and his family, without it causing him one
qualm of regret.

The more he saw of the women who had made
London, under the Prince of Wales, who was now the
Regent, the gayest and one of the most promiscuous
cities in the world, the more he was determined that
love-affairs were one thing but marriage was most
certainly another.

He had no intention of marrying a woman who
would be unfaithful to him and he disliked the idea
of having to deceive his wife, having to lie in an
effort to protect himself.

He knew that he was too proud and had too much
integrity to wish to debase himself in any way, least
of all by falsehood and deception.

"I shall never marry," the Duke had said not once
but a thousand times.

He thought now that it would be a pity if he could
no longer indulge in such delightful intrigues as the
one which had happened last night without experi-
encing a somewhat guilty conscience the following
morning.

As it was, he imagined with amusement that either
the Tsar or someone in the Foreign Ministry would
undoubtedly be asking Katharina what she had learnt
from him the night before.

And although he was certain that with her agile
mind she would give them something to chew over,

he had in fact said nothing that could not be published in any Russian newspaper which existed.

He had seen Katharina in the distance today at luncheon, looking alluringly attractive in a gown that was definitely Parisian and wearing fantastic jewels which he was certain had not been given to her by her aged and fortunately absent husband.

Their eyes had met for one moment across the Reception-Room into which they had moved when the meal was over.

Without words she told the Duke that she wanted him and he had only to lift his finger for her to be at his side.

What she signalled, however, made the Duke decide that before he concerned himself once again with their fiery love-making, he should extend his knowledge of St. Petersburg and perhaps find out from outside the Palace what other people were thinking.

Accordingly, he now went down the magnificent marble stairway with its white and gold pillars to the front door.

Here he ordered one of the *drotskis,* which were always at the disposal of the Tsar's guests, and, having given instructions to be taken to the Ysevolsov Palace, set off in the sunshine.

Even for August it was very hot and there was little breeze coming from the river, although there was a touch of salt in the air.

The enormously wide roads laid out by Peter the Great had practically no traffic on them at this time of the day, when most people preferred to remain at home, and anyway, owing to the ominous news of Napoleon's advance, there was less entertaining than usual.

As he drove along, the Duke enjoyed looking at the magnificent Palaces and other buildings, which were so different in their brilliant colours from the grey Palladians of England.

The Roumainzov Palace was painted orange, the Ministry of Justice was blue, and the enormous Pavlovski Barracks, designed for Tsar Paul, was yellow.

The Duke was most interested in the *Manège* of the Garde à cheval. It was painted green and had a portico of eight white-granite Doric columns.

With his great knowledge of horse-flesh the Duke had already admired the black horses of the Garde à cheval, the chestnuts of the Chevaliers Gardes, and the dapple greys of the Gatchina Hussars.

The *drotski,* drawn by two excellent horses, reached the Ysevolsov Palace within five minutes.

The Duke entered the Hallway, and if it was not as magnificent as that in the Winter Palace, it could certainly stand comparison with any house he had visited elsewhere in the world.

A flunkey took him up the marble staircase, which divided and rose to a landing ornamented with exquisite specimens of Chinese porcelain.

They passed through a Reception-Room so large that two hundred people or more could easily be entertained in it without crowding.

The Duke expected to be asked to wait, but the flunkey, speaking in hesitating French, explained:

"*Madame la Princesse* is in the Theatre, *Monsieur.*"

The Duke nodded his understanding and they walked on again, through a number of magnificently decorated rooms, until in the centre of one of them they reached a staircase made of priceless malachite descending to the floor below.

The Duke had heard in England that Prince Ysevolsov's private Theatre was exceptional, but he was not prepared for the beauty of what he saw when the servant opened a gold-encrusted door and he was shown into what was obviously a Royal Box.

Very small, in fact holding fewer than a hundred people, it was like a child's doll's-house in a Royal Mansion, and yet it had all the charm and beauty of an Imperial Theatre.

In the stalls there were white and gold carved chairs, and the circle was supplied with seats upholstered in crimson velvet, as was the Box he had entered.

The flunkey had not announced him and he stood at the back, noting in front of him the figure of the Princess, who had not heard his arrival because she was intent on watching what was taking place on the stage.

A girl was dancing to the music of a small Orchestra seated in the pit below.

The Duke glanced at the performer perfunctorily. He assumed that with the Prince's obsession for the Theatre, it would be either a member of his own special *Corps de Ballet* giving a performance, or, which was more likely, one of his family.

At the back of his mind he remembered the Princess or someone else telling him that the Prince himself enjoyed acting and expected his family to perform with him.

If there was one thing the Duke really disliked it was amateur theatricals, and he hoped that what was taking place would not continue too long, as he wanted to talk to the Princess.

Then the girl who was dancing made a deep curtsey.

'Thank goodness!' the Duke thought to himself.

He was just about to move forward to make his presence known to his hostess as the girl, and he could see that she was very pretty, ran from the stage, and then the music changed and another performer appeared.

She was moving on the tips of her toes and wearing the traditional ballet-skirt worn by those who took part in *La Sylphide*.

It reached to her ankles, and there was a tight bodice, low-cut to display her long, swan-like neck and bare arms.

The Duke thought impatiently that the new Ballet which he had seen performed the preceding evening, in Catherine the Great's Theatre in the Winter Palace, rather bored him.

Then he realised that this was not the music of that Ballet and he had not heard it before, and also that the movements of the dancer on the stage were exceptionally graceful.

Despite his irritation, he found himself watching the way she moved.

He had a feeling that the dance was not traditional, but if it was, he had never seen it before.

He knew too that the music, while strange, was particularly tuneful and had about it a melodious beauty that intrigued him.

The Duke, like the Prince Regent, was very fond of music.

As in everything else in which he was interested, he was a connoisseur and a very discriminating one.

Now he knew that he was listening to an exceptionally fine work which did not sound to him in the least Russian.

Then as he watched the girl moving round the stage, dancing with a spontaneity and a kind of joy that he had never seen expressed before, he was sure, although he had no reason for it, that she too was unusual.

He could not explain why she seemed different, except that as far as he was concerned, she was original in her movements, in her grace, and in her dance.

'Russia is full of surprises!' he thought to himself, and found that the music of the dance evoked a response in him that he had not felt for a very long time.

Earlier, when he was young, he had been deeply moved, not only by music but also by poetry, until, like everything else in his life, it had grown too familiar. He had found that while he appreciated the subtleties of such things, they no longer aroused him as they had when he was young.

Now, strangely, almost inexplicably, he felt his mind —or was it something deeper?—flying as if it had wings to the music, while his eyes watched the grace and joy expressed by the dancer.

It seemed to him as if she moved amongst trees covered with blossoms and the whole world awakened with spring.

There was something young and creative about her, and the Duke thought that he saw butterflies hovering round her and birds in the sky above.

It was almost with a sense of loss that he realised that the performance was over as the dancer swept to the ground in the traditional curtsey and the music came to an end.

Two red velvet curtains fell, then rose as the two girls came forward hand-in-hand to take a final bow.

There was only the Princess to clap her hands, but she did so with enthusiasm.

"Excellent!" she called out. "Both of you were very good! Go and change and come to the White Salon."

The two girls slipped away through the curtains, and for the first time the Princess became aware that the Duke was standing behind her in the Box.

She gave a little cry of delight and, rising, held out both her hands.

"Blake!" she cried. "You have come, and I am so very pleased to see you!"

"As I to see you, Sonya," the Duke answered. "Who were those entrancing creatures? They held me spell-bound."

"The first was Tania, my little Tania, whom I so much want you to meet," the Princess replied. "You will see her in a few moments, and I know you will believe everything I have told you about her, and so much more."

The Princess linked her arm through the Duke's as she spoke and led him through the door at the back of the Box.

As they started to climb the malachite staircase, the Duke asked:

"And the other dancer?"

There was a quite perceptible pause before the Princess replied:

"Oh, that was Zoia!"

Chapter Two

The Duke was about to ask Zoia's surname, but the Princess chattered on:

"You must find it terribly hot, as we all do. Of course, ordinarily we are never in St. Petersburg at this time of year, but as the Tsar is at the Winter Palace, how can we go to the country and feel that we are deserting him?"

They were moving through the beautiful apartments which the Duke had noted on his way to the Theatre, and as the flunkeys opened the double doors of a huge Reception-Room, the Duke realised that the White Salon was aptly named as it was in fact all white.

The carved stone mantelpiece was an artistic delight and the curtains beneath the exquisite gold pelmets were of heavy white Chinese silk.

There was a glittering silver tea-pot on a silver tray set on a low table by one of the sofas, and the Princess laughed when she saw the Duke's expression.

"English tea at five o'clock," she said. "I became acclimatised to it in England and now quite a number

of people in St. Petersburg have followed my example.
I cannot offer you muffins, but I think you will find
the little *blini* to your taste."

As these were, the Duke knew, small buckwheat
pancakes filled with caviare and sour-cream, he could
reply quite truthfully that they were very much to his
taste.

He sat down in a comfortable chair and waited for
the cup of tea that the Princess poured out in the
same manner as that in which his mother had dis-
pensed tea in England.

"How long are you staying?" she asked. "Or have
you not yet made up your mind?"

"I rather feel that the news from the Front might
decide that for me," the Duke replied.

The Princess shrugged her shoulders.

"Now that we have Kutuzov, everything will be
all right and our Army will win!"

The Duke thought she was being slightly over-
optimistic, but at least it was a change from the
despondency at the Winter Palace, so he merely answered:

"I hope you are right. You should come and talk to
the Tsar."

"It would do no good," the Princess replied. "You
know as well as I do, Blake, that if there is one thing
the Russians really enjoy, it is gloom and despondency whenever there is a crisis. My husband is just
the same, but with him I merely wait until the sun
shines again."

The Duke laughed.

"An easy philosophy," he said, "from a very lovely
philosopher."

There was no doubt that he spoke the truth when
he complimented the Princess.

She had been, when the Prince had married her,

the most outstanding beauty in the Court of Vienna, and age had improved rather than detracted from her looks.

There was, however, a forcefulness about her which made the Duke suspect that she drove her husband and in a very un-Russian manner ruled the house.

Russians for the most part liked their women to be soft, feminine, and unobtrusive, but the two famous Empresses, Elizabeth and Catherine, had set a standard which many Russian wives followed by being irritatingly dictatorial.

The Princess, however, was not Russian, and the Duke knew that it amused her to decry the nation into which she had married simply because she wished to challenge her husband's importance.

The Prince was a good-natured, easy-going man. He liked peace in his home and peace for his country, and the Duke was certain that if he was playing the part of a soldier at the moment, it was reluctantly and only from a sense of patriotism.

The Princess was talking about London and asking questions about her friends when the door opened and the two girls whom the Duke had seen dancing came into the room.

There was no doubt that Tania, who led the way, was as pretty as her mother had described her.

She had very dark hair and white skin, large eyes set well apart, and a full, smiling mouth.

As she curtseyed to the Duke, he was sure that when she went to London she would be a social success.

Then he heard the Princess say:

"And this is Zoia. She came with us from Moscow so that Tania could improve her French."

For the first time since she had entered the room the Duke looked at the girl whom he had seen danc-

ing on the stage and who had mysteriously affected
him in a manner which he did not wish to remember.

He was sure that it had been just an illusion, en-
gendered by the heat of the day or perhaps by a
delayed reaction to the wine he had drunk at luncheon.

Whatever the cause, he did not wish to recall it,
and he had been quite certain that when he met Zoia
face to face he would realise that it was just a fantasy
of his mind and in fact had little to do with the performance.

A slight figure curtseyed gracefully in front of him.

Then as she rose, she lifted her face to his and he
found himself looking into eyes that seemed in some
extraordinary way to have purple depths in them.

As he looked at Zoia's face the Duke realised that
she was different from any other woman he had ever
met before.

It was not that she was beautiful—a great many
women were that. It was not that she was particularly
striking. In fact, her loveliness was not so obvious as
that of Tania.

But there was something in the almost classical features, the straight little nose, the perfect curve of the
lips, the oval of the face, which reminded the Duke
of the statuary he had seen in Greece and of some of
the very fine examples that he himself owned amongst
his other treasures.

He thought too as he looked at her that while she
was flesh and blood, she had the purity and the ex-
clusiveness of the statues which had once been wor-
shipped by those who appreciated their sanctity.

That, he told himself in an almost startled manner,
was the right word to describe Zoia.

There was in fact something sacred about her, and
he thought for one moment that there was a light be-

hind her or coming from within her as she stood facing him.

He realised that they were looking at each other, that Zoia's eyes were held by his, and that both of them were very still.

The Princess's voice seemed to come from a long way away.

"Sit down, children," she said, "and hurry with your tea. I want to talk to His Grace, who is a very old friend, and we prefer to be alone."

She was pouring tea into a cup as she spoke, and now she looked up and was aware that the Duke and Zoia had not moved.

In a voice that had a sharp edge to it she added:

"I am sure, Zoia, it is time for you to practise your music. Go to the Music-Room and tell the servants to bring your tea there. It will save time."

As the Princess spoke, Zoia gave a start as if she had been recalled from some distant place.

She gave the Princess a little curtsey, then without speaking went from the room.

As the door shut behind her, the Duke had a sudden desire to call out to her to stay, and when she had gone, he had an unaccountable feeling of loss because she was no longer there.

"Come and sit down, Blake," the Princess begged, "and tell my little Tania about London. She has not been there since she was ten, but she has the happiest memories of your Parks and the funny, narrow little streets."

The Duke realised that the Princess's description of London was due to the fact that the streets of St. Petersburg were so wide and so sparsely inhabited.

Because Tania was looking at him in an expectant manner, he asked genially:

"Are you really looking forward to visiting London?

I can assure you it is not half so grand and impressive as St. Petersburg."

"Mama tells me I shall attend Balls in London which are more amusing than those that take place here."

"That I find difficult to believe," the Duke replied, "with so many handsome and dashing young officers to partner you."

"Not at the moment," Tania answered. "They are all away fighting the French and there are far too many women at every party."

As she spoke she pouted, and the Duke laughed.

"Let us hope then, for your sake if for nobody else's, that the war will be over soon."

"War! War! War!" the Princess said, groaning. "Do we ever hear of anything else? I had planned such delightful parties for Tania at the Summer Palace and now all we can do is to stay here in this heat."

"I can only say how sorry I am for you," the Duke said with a slight cynical note in his voice.

He thought it was typical of the Princess to ignore the huge casualties there had been at the Battle of Smolensk.

"Let us talk of something more interesting," the Princess said with a swift change of mood before he could speak. "Now that you are here, I must give a party for you—a dinner-party—and we will dance afterwards to a new Gypsy Band I have discovered which is quite fantastic."

She smiled before she added:

"I am keeping them secret in case they should appear at a party before mine, but you shall be my excuse to present them to an astonished St. Petersburg."

"Will the Tsar approve?" the Duke asked. "After all, he is very depressed and worried about the war."

"We will not invite him," the Princess said. "We will tell everyone that it is just a quiet little dinner-party for you, but all my special friends shall come, and Tania and I will entertain you, will we not, dearest?"

She spoke to Tania, whose eyes were alight with excitement.

"A party with dancing afterwards, Mama! It will be so thrilling! I was saying to Zoia only today how dull it is with nothing to look forward to."

"You have your Ballet-dancing," the Duke reminded her.

Tania shrugged her shoulders.

"I have had lessons for years to please Papa," she said, "but Zoia dances so much better than I do."

"Zoia comes into another category altogether," the Princess said coldly. "Now run along, darling, and I will let you come back and say good-bye to the Duke before he leaves."

"I should like that," Tania said, with what was almost a coquettish glance at the Duke.

She curtseyed and ran from the room and the Princess watched her go. Then she asked:

"What do you think of her, Blake?"

"I think she is extremely pretty, like her mother," the Duke replied, "and she will be a triumphant success amongst the Beaux of St. James's."

"I would like her to be a success with you," the Princess said softly.

"Me?" the Duke enquired in a voice which proclaimed that he had never thought of such an idea. "You know that I am a confirmed bachelor! Besides, I am much too old for anything so young and lovely."

"I think Tania would be happier with an older man," the Princess said seriously. "She needs guidance. She also at times needs a firm hand."

"Have you ever wondered what I should have in common with a child who has only just left the School-Room?" the Duke asked. "No, my dear Sonya, my interests are very much more sophisticated."

He deliberately spoke in a way that made it a compliment, and there was, as he had intended, a sudden alertness in the Princess's eyes as she put out one of her heavily ringed hands towards him.

"You know as well as I do, Blake," she said, "that you typify everything that is handsome, gallant, and attractive in an Englishman."

The Duke kissed her fingers, as was expected, then said:

"I promise you that all the most eligible bachelors shall be paraded before Tania when you bring her to London. In fact, I think one of my younger brothers might suit her very well."

As he spoke he saw that the Princess was calculating that if he never married, as he said he had no intention of doing, then his brother would, in time, become the Duke of Welminster and Tania would achieve the position she wished for her.

Aloud she merely said:

"I knew I could rely on your kindness."

"Tell me about Tania's friend," the Duke asked. "She also seems to be quite a pretty girl. Will you be bringing her to London too?"

He deliberately made his voice sound uninterested, and the Princess replied:

"Poor Zoia, I am so sorry for her. It is not her fault that things are as they are."

"What do you mean by that?" the Duke asked, again in what he hoped was an uninterested voice.

"I forgot," the Princess said, "that I did not tell you who she was."

"And who is she?"

"She is Pierre Vallon's daughter."

For a moment the Duke could not think where he had heard the name.

Then he exclaimed:

"Do you mean the Conductor?"

"Of course!" the Princess replied. "There is only one Vallon in the Music World, and he now has a unique position."

"I heard him conducting in London last year," the Duke said, "and long ago when I was a boy in Paris. I suppose he is without exception one of the greatest Conductors in the world today, and I have always thought the music he composes is superlative."

As he spoke, he knew now why he had been so drawn to the music to which Zoia had danced and which had aroused such strange feelings within him.

"I had no idea that Vallon had a family," he added.

"You know his story, of course," the Princess said.

"As a matter of fact, I do not," the Duke replied. "I have admired and acclaimed him for his art, but I suppose I never thought of him as a man."

"Then I will tell you," the Princess said.

The Duke knew that because she was an insatiable gossip, it pleased her to be able to impart to him something he did not know already.

"Pierre Vallon's wife," she said, "was Natasha Strovolsky."

The Duke was startled, as she had meant him to be.

"Strovolsky!" he exclaimed.

He was well aware that the Strovolsky family, one of the most important in Russia, were extremely proud of their Royal connections.

Wherever the Tsar went there was always one member of the family in attendance upon him, by right not only as a Courtier but by birth because the same blood flowed in their veins.

The Strovolskys were so proud, so Imperial in their behaviour, that it was often laughingly said that the Tsar would wake up one morning to find a Strovolsky sitting on the throne!

Without the Princess saying any-more, the Duke knew that the idea of a member of the Strovolsky family marrying a French Conductor, however famous, was unthinkable.

"How can it be possible?" he asked.

He knew that the Princess was only waiting for the question to begin her story.

"You will remember," she began, "that it was Grigori Orlov who put Catherine II on the throne of Russia."

"Yes, of course," the Duke murmured.

Count Orlov, as he became, was part of Russian history.

He was extremely handsome and insatiably ambitious, and in 1762 Europe learnt with astonishment that due to his machinations, a German Princess of petty origin had snatched the Crown of Russia first from Tsar Peter III and then from Peter's son Paul. The Duke had heard her described as "not only a murderess but a usurper; not only a usurper but a whore."

The Duke's father, who had visited Russia at that time, had often told him how obsessed the Empress, an autocrat with everyone else, had been with her lover Orlov.

"I believe the fellow beats her in private," the old Duke had said, "but she is passionately in love with him, and I have never seen anything like the presents that have been heaped upon him."

The Duke remembered now that his father had described a suit the Count had worn on which was sewn a million pounds' worth of diamonds and told him of a fete at which the dessert at supper was set out with jewels to the value of over two million pounds sterling.

"Ten years after her Coronation," the Princess now continued, "the Empress Catherine decided to replace Grigori Orlov as her lover."

The Duke smiled.

"Because he was having an affair with Princess Golitsyna."

"Exactly!" the Princess agreed. "But what the Empress did not know, nor at the time did anyone else, was that he had also been briefly but passionately in love with the young Princess Petya Strovolsky!"

"It seems incredible!" the Duke exclaimed.

"Incredible or not, you can imagine the horror when they discovered that their prettiest and most adored daughter was having a child."

The Princess made a gesture with her hands that was very eloquent before she continued:

"The Prince was an astute and of course allpowerful man. Very, very few people, and only those closest to the family, were aware of this lamentable and indeed, from their point of view, horrifying situation. They were not only humiliated by the position but terrified, as you can imagine, that the Empress would learn of it."

"What did they do?" the Duke asked.

"Petya was sent to stay with some friends in Austria, which is how I came to learn the sad story," the Princess said. "Her child was born there, and it was a daughter who was christened Natasha."

The Duke was listening intently as the Princess went on:

"A year later Petya and the baby returned to Russia and the Strovolskys accepted the baby, announcing that Petya had married a distant cousin who had died in Vienna."

"And they were believed?" the Duke enquired.

"But of course!" the Princess answered. "No-one would dare to contradict any statement made by Prince Strovolsky."

"Then what happened?" the Duke asked.

"Natasha was brought up with the family. Petya married one of my husband's cousins and died in childbirth. Count Orlov was the love of her life. She never really cared for anybody else."

"I believe the Empress reinstated him, did she not?" the Duke asked.

"She always said: 'I cannot be a day without love,' for as a lover she missed him desperately. On his return she loaded him with gifts, six thousand serfs, a salary of one hundred fifty thousand roubles, and Heaven knows what else."

"Am I mistaken in thinking that he gave her a gift of great importance?" the Duke asked.

"A superb solitaire diamond," the Princess replied. "It cost him four hundred and sixty thousand roubles. It is the most beautiful single gem in the world!"

The Duke registered in his mind that in the Empress Catherine's reign, five roubles equalled one British pound, so Orlov's gift was certainly an expressive apology.

"Go on with your story," he begged.

"You can imagine the consternation in the Strovolsky household, after they had done everything they could to try to forget the anxiety and the risk of humiliation and shame that Petya had brought upon them, to discover that Petya's daughter, Natasha, had run away with their children's tutor."

"So that was what Pierre Vallon was!"

"He came to Russia, like so many other Frenchmen, to teach the children of the noble families to speak, to dance, and to make music," the Princess replied. "You have seen him and therefore will understand that anyone who employed such a handsome man in a household full of young girls was asking for trouble."

The Duke agreed.

He had thought that Pierre Vallon, when he had seen him conducting at a huge party given by the Prince of Wales at Carlton House, was not only outstandingly good-looking but had an inescapable charm that had made the ladies present fawn on him in a manner which had made their host quite jealous.

"What did Princess Natasha look like?" he asked.

"She was absolutely lovely!" the Princess replied.

"Was?" the Duke questioned.

"She died a year ago; that is why I am so sorry for Zoia and brought her here from Moscow while her father is conducting at the Grand Theatre, to give her a chance to forget what is inevitably a worse tragedy than it would be for any other girl in similar circumstances."

"Why do you say that?" the Duke asked.

The Princess looked at him pityingly, as if he was being rather stupid.

"While the Princess was alive," she replied, "the child had some chance of meeting decent men, one of whom might have been inclined to ignore the social consequences of marrying her, but now . . ."

The Princess's hands went out expressively.

"Now, Zoia is just the daughter of a French Conductor."

"But a very famous one," the Duke said, "and a Composer whose work rates with that of the greatest Masters of music."

"However talented he may be," the Princess said coldly, "however delightful to meet, you know as well as I do, my dear Blake, that socially he is just a French tutor who has achieved success in his own particular profession."

She sighed.

"I am very sorry for Zoia, and I am certain that now that Natasha is dead, the Strovolskys will no longer wish to know her—in fact they have already told me so. I cannot believe that she will find Paris very amusing at this moment, with Bonaparte conscripting every eligible man over the age of fifteen into his infamous Army."

"I can see the position very clearly," the Duke remarked.

"Now you understand how charitable I have been in having her here at all," the Princess said. "Tania is fond of her, and at least the two girls amuse each other when there is so little entertainment taking place at the moment."

As if she was bored with the subject of Zoia, the Princess went on:

"Now let us make plans, Blake. Which evening can you escape from the Palace? But give me a little time to make it a really festive occasion."

"I have the feeling we will be in the Tsar's 'black book.'"

"Then tell someone to give him another Bible to read!" the Princess retorted. "It is all over St. Petersburg that Prince Golitzin has got him immersed in the Holy Scriptures. Personally, I am waiting until I am ready for the grave before I become really religious."

Before the Duke could reply, a servant came into the room and said something in a low voice to the Princess.

"Oh, what a nuisance!" she exclaimed. "There is a Courier here from my husband, not only bringing me news from the Front but requiring a number of papers which only I can find."

The Duke rose to his feet.

"Then I must leave you," he said. "If you are writing to the Prince, please tell him how disappointed I am that we cannot meet."

"He will be disappointed too," the Princess replied. "He has always been fond of you, as you are well aware."

She waved the servant away and said to the Duke in a low voice:

"Come and see me tomorrow and we will make plans. Also, I have a lot to tell you for which there is no time now."

She spoke in a way which made the Duke look at her enquiringly.

Then, having glanced over her shoulder to make sure that the servant had left the room, she said in a low voice:

"Be careful of Katharina Bagration."

"Careful?" the Duke asked.

"She is very close to the Tsar, and it is well known that she helps the Foreign Ministry with their investigations."

The Duke was too polite to say that he knew this already.

"Thank you, dear Sonya," he said. "You have always been a kind and generous friend, and I assure you I am very grateful."

He raised her hand to his lips and kissed it.

The Duke walked from the room to see waiting outside the door the Courier who had come from the Prince, wearing a stained and dusty uniform and looking as if he had ridden a long distance without sleep.

As the servant showed the Courier into the White Salon, the Duke walked along the corridor in the direction of the staircase.

He had reached it and was just about to descend

the stairs when he heard the sound of music coming from a room on the other side of the landing.

He hesitated for a moment, then walked to the door and opened it.

The room was as magnificent as the others in the house.

There were huge pillars of a very rare marble which supported an exquisitely painted oval ceiling, and the walls were decorated with murals of goddesses and cupids.

On a small platform there was a pianoforte and seated at it was Zoia, playing a melody which the Duke seemed to recognise.

He entered the room, shutting the door behind him, and walked slowly towards her, and it seemed to him once again that she was enveloped with light.

She was so intent on what she was playing that only when he drew nearer did she glance up and see him.

She stopped playing but she did not rise, and once again their eyes met and it seemed as if neither of them could move.

At last, after what seemed to be a very long time, the Duke found his voice.

"Is that one of your father's compositions?"

"Yes."

Her voice was very low and he thought it had exactly the tone that he might have expected of her.

"I have met your father."

There was a sudden brightness in her eyes, almost as if they held the sunshine.

It was strange, the Duke thought, that her hair should be fair.

Then he remembered that Pierre Vallon was not dark like most Frenchmen, and he imagined, although he was not sure, that he came from Normandy, where fair hair and blue eyes were as common as they were in England.

There was no doubt that Zoia must have her mother's eyes, and yet they had none of the mystery which the Duke had always associated with Russian women.

Instead, there was something which, like her face, had a spiritual quality which was inescapable.

He walked forward to step onto the small dais and lean against the piano.

"Tell me about yourself," he said.

She smiled.

"What do you wish to know?"

"How have you learnt to dance as I saw you dancing just now on the stage?"

She did not appear surprised and he thought that she must have seen him in the Box when she and Tania took their bows in front of the curtain.

"When I was small," Zoia said, "Mama and I used to watch Papa play for the *Corps de Ballet*."

"You went to the Theatre?"

"Yes . . . in Paris or anywhere else where he was playing," she replied. "Mama always wanted to be with him and he liked her to be there."

Without her having to say any more, the Duke knew that there had been a deep love between her father and mother.

He could understand that because the Princess had given up so much for her love, she wanted always to be with the man who mattered to her more than all the pomp and circumstance that she had enjoyed in Russia.

"Because I wanted to dance like the ladies in the Ballet," Zoia was saying, "Mama arranged for me to have lessons from a famous Ballerina who had retired."

"You dance very beautifully."

"I would like to believe that it is true," Zoia replied, "but Papa's music which he wrote for me is so inspiring that when I hear it played I feel as if I am swept away into another world, where there is only music and sunshine."

That is exactly what she had portrayed with her dancing, the Duke thought, and he remembered how he had thought he saw butterflies and birds fluttering round her and felt that she danced under the blossoms of the trees.

Even as he remembered it, he was startled to realise that what he must have been seeing was what was in Zoia's thoughts.

Almost as if he would confirm or refute the idea out-of-hand, he asked:

"Tell me—tell me exactly what you were thinking just now when I watched you dancing."

She did not seem surprised at his question. She merely looked away from him, and he thought that she was not only racking her memory to recall what was happening but staring deep into her heart.

"That particular music of Papa's, which is part of a Concerto," she said, "makes me think of . . . spring . . . the blossoms on the trees, the birds nesting, and the flowers and the butterflies hovering over them."

The Duke was silent from sheer astonishment. Then he said:

"I understand that your mother is dead. What will you do with yourself when you leave St. Petersburg?"

"I have come only for a short visit," Zoia answered, "because Papa asked me to do so, but today I heard for the first time that the French Army may be marching towards Moscow."

"It is a possibility."

"Then I must be with Papa."

"Your father will be safe, whoever is in Moscow,"

the Duke said soothingly. "Pierre Vallon is an international figure and music, as you know, has no nationality but is universal."

"That is true," Zoia said with a smile. "At the same time, guns do not always hit the target at which they are aimed, and if there was fighting in Moscow I should be very frightened that Papa might be injured."

"Do you think if you are with him you will be able to prevent that?" the Duke enquired.

"I shall pray that he will be safe," Zoia replied. "At the same time, I wish to be at his side."

"I think it would be far better if your father came to St. Petersburg," the Duke said. "But I will find out exactly what the situation is when I return to the Palace, and I will let your hostess know."

"That is very kind of you."

She gave a little sigh.

"Perhaps I was wrong to come away and leave Papa alone, but he was so insistent that I should accept the Princess's kind invitation."

"You are happy here?" the Duke enquired.

He did not miss the perceptibly little pause before Zoia said:

"I like being with Tania . . . she is a very sweet person."

Although her voice was warm, she spoke almost as if Tania were a child and she was looking after her.

"How old are you?" the Duke asked.

"I am nearly twenty!"

It struck the Duke that in twenty years she must have seen in her travels with her father and mother a great deal of the world, and therefore would in fact be very much older in mind and in knowledge than were her contemporaries.

"Play to me," he suggested.

"What would you like to hear?"

"Something your father wrote," he replied, "and something that is your favourite too."

Zoia ran her fingers over the keys.

Her hands were small and perfectly proportioned, and as she looked down, her eye-lashes were dark against her cheeks.

The Duke thought she resembled even more than she had done before the statues which had always aroused in him a more intimate response than pictures.

He had in his possession some of the finest pictures in England painted by great artists from every country in Europe, but whenever he returned to one of his houses, it was his statuary that delighted him most.

Now he thought that the Aphrodite which stood in his house in Hampshire, and which had been brought back centuries ago from Greece by one of his ancestors, was more like Zoia than were any of his canvasses of the Madonna, Venus, or angels.

As she began to play, the Duke knew that incredibly, in a manner which he could not begin to understand, he was reading her thoughts and feeling within himself her response to the music.

It was winter and the Duke could see the snow on the ground, the trees white with frost, and a stretch of frozen water.

It was beautiful but cold, impersonal, apart from human needs.

Then, imperceptibly, so that for a moment one sensed rather than saw it, the sky brightened.

There was light, then the first glimmer of sun, and slowly the snow melted, the still blue ice broke and became a moving stream, the frost fell from the trees, and the branches came to life.

Now there were the green buds of spring and the first white snowdrops and crocuses in the grass beneath them.

It was all in the rhythm and the smooth melody of the music, and yet to the Duke it was as vivid as if he saw it happening in front of him. He could almost feel the warmth of the sunshine, smell the scent of the flowers as they bloomed one after another, and see the blossoms fashion themselves in the trees.

Then there was not only nature in what he saw, but someone human coming through the trees and moving towards him, and he knew that she sought him as he waited for her.

She came nearer and nearer and as she did so he felt that his whole being went out towards her.

As he reached out, not only with his arms but with his very soul, everything vanished.

There was silence, and with a start that seemed to shake his whole body, he realised that Zoia, sitting at the piano, was looking at him, her hands in her lap.

"Did you . . . like it . . . Your Grace?"

There was just a touch of anxiety in her soft voice, as if she found it hard to understand why he had not spoken and why he was looking at her so strangely.

"Very—much!"

The Duke heard his voice coming as if from a long distance away.

"I am glad . . . but I do not play as well as . . . Papa does."

"What does your father—call it?"

It was still very difficult for the Duke to speak. He felt as if his voice was constrained and was no longer his own.

"Papa called it 'The Melting of the Ice,' " Zoia answered. "There is a great deal more of the composition . . . but I thought perhaps you might be . . . bored."

The Duke wanted to say that she had no right to

stop when she had. He had wanted her to go on. He had wanted to know what would happen when he touched the person for whom he had been waiting.

Then he told himself that if he said such a thing, she would think he was mad. And yet he was not sure —she might understand.

He realised that she was waiting for him to say something, but before he could speak, she said:

"I think you . . . understood what Papa was . . . trying to say."

"Why should you think that?" he enquired.

"I do not know exactly," she replied simply. "But while I was playing I felt that it was not . . . just the music you heard . . . but something else."

Quite suddenly the Duke felt that he was bewitched, and he was not sure that he liked it.

"I must go," he said sharply. "Thank you, Miss Vallon, for playing for me. I am sure your father must be very proud of you."

Even as he spoke he knew that he had disappointed her, but she politely rose to her feet and curtseyed.

"Good-bye!" he said.

He wanted to go and yet he wanted to stay. He did not understand himself.

"Good-bye . . . Your Grace!"

The words were very low and she did not look at him.

There was so much he wanted to ask, and yet he did not wish to hear the answers.

Abruptly, because he had been disturbed out of his usual calm, blasé attitude, he walked across the room towards the door.

Only as he reached it did he look back to see that Zoia was still standing at the piano.

She was not looking after him, as any other woman would have done. Instead, she was staring down at the keyboard, and once again he had the feeling that he had disappointed her.

He went from the room, closing the door behind him.

As he walked down the stairs he told himself again that everything he had felt was an illusion and something to do with the heat.

His *drotski* was waiting, and as he drove back towards the Winter Palace he thought that in some strange manner he had become immersed in the emotional dramatics of the Russians, who veered from elation to depression like a seesaw.

Yet that explanation did not hold good, because in fact he was neither depressed nor elated.

Instead, he had only felt something so strange that he could not explain it even to himself.

It had startled him out of a complacency in which for some years he had believed that there was nothing new under the sun and certainly nothing emotional that he had not tried in one way or another.

"I can hardly be becoming psychic in my old age!" the Duke said to himself almost savagely.

It was fashionable in London to consult fortune-tellers and mediums, and the Duke had heard that both Napoleon and his wife, Josephine, were fanatically superstitious.

It was well known that when the Empress had been a girl in Martinique she had been told that she would "occupy the highest position in France."

English Generals would relate scornfully that Napoleon consulted sooth-sayers before he embarked on a battle and was not above taking his revenge on anyone who predicted bad luck.

The Duke had always thought that all such omens were "a lot of nonsense" practised only by charlatans who wished to obtain money in a fraudulent manner.

Over the years he had stayed at various houses which were reputed to be haunted by ghosts, and on more than one occasion he had occupied what was known as the "Ghost Room."

"How did you sleep?" his host would ask breathlessly when the Duke appeared at breakfast-time.

"Absolutely peacefully!" he would reply with relish. "I was not disturbed the whole night. In fact, your ghost took not the slightest interest in me!"

His attitude was always deflating to his hosts, and he was equally contemptuous of all those who carried talismans at race-meetings and those of the theatrical profession who insisted on having hare's-feet in their dressing-rooms.

"Good or bad luck is all in the mind," he had said often enough. "We make our fate, and our destiny is in our own hands."

Now he asked himself how it was possible that he of all people could be beguiled not once but twice not exactly into seeing a vision but into feeling someone else's thoughts.

He was aware of them to the point where they were as real to him as the setting sun gleaming iridescent on the waters of the Neva River and the statues on the roof of the Winter Palace silhouetted against the evening sky.

"I am either drunk or going mad!" the Duke told himself irritably.

But he knew that it was neither of these things.

'The sooner I forget such nonsense and get down to work, the better!' he thought as he stepped out of the *drotski* and went up the steps and into the Winter Palace.

He decided that he would find out what was the latest news from the Front and spend at least an hour coding a long communiqué to Lord Castlereagh in London.

A Courier could take it from him first thing in the morning, and at least he would justify his stay in St. Petersburg.

He walked into the Hall and handed his hat to an attendant flunkey. Then an Officer of the Grenadiers of the Golden Guard, who were on duty in the Hall and along the corridors, came towards him.

"Good-evening, Your Grace," he said in French. "The Princess Katharina Bagration would be grateful if you could visit her before you retire to your rooms."

"Of course," the Duke replied. "I shall be delighted to see Her Highness."

The Officer instructed a servant to escort the Duke to the Princess's apartments.

As he followed the Officer, the Duke thought that Katharina would bring him down to earth and disperse all his ridiculous fantasies.

The one thing about Katharina was that she was very human—passionate, fiery, demanding, which were all emotions which the Duke could understand, feelings of which he was thoroughly cognisant.

'That is what I want,' he thought to himself, 'and nothing—no, nothing else!'

Chapter Three

The Duke half-expected to find Katharina alone, but when the flunkey showed him into a large, important Reception-Room redolent with flowers, he found that there were a number of other people present.

Katharina, looking extremely beautiful in a gown of blue gauze, moved towards him and he knew by the expression in her eyes how pleased she was to see him.

He kissed her hand, then went immediately to greet the Tsarina, who was present with the Tsar.

Elisabeth Feodorovna would have been an extremely attractive and fitting mate for the handsome Alexander, but unfortunately she had a most unbecoming scurvy on her face.

The Duke, however, had always found her charming and far more emotionally stable than her husband.

He had spoken to her for only a few minutes when the Tsar interrupted them.

"I have something to tell you, Welminster," he said, leading the Duke a little aside from the other people in the room.

The Duke looked at him apprehensively but thought

52

he seemed in a far better mood than he had been yesterday.

The despondency which always made him seem to
shrink into himself and become less imposing had
gone, and instead he was the commanding figure that
he appeared to the Russians when he was on parade.

"What is it, Sire?" the Duke asked.

"I know that all will be well," the Tsar replied impressively. "Russia will conquer Napoleon, and there
is no longer any need for alarm."

The Duke looked at him incredulously, and the
Tsar went on:

"This morning I had a direct message which told
me that my fears, my anxiety, had been quite ground-
less."

"A message from the Front, Sire?"

"No, from God Himself," the Tsar replied.

The Duke waited, wondering if anyone in England
would believe this conversation if he recounted it in a
despatch.

"I passed a night of terrible apprehension," the Tsar
began, "until at dawn I went to the window to look
out, and a voice told me to search in my Bible for in-
spiration."

He took a deep breath as if he was remembering
exactly what had happened.

"I put my finger into the Holy Book," he continued,
"and it pointed to a phrase which answered all my
problems in a few words."

"What did it say, Sire?" the Duke asked, knowing
that the question was expected of him.

" 'Arise and shine, for thy light is come and the glory
of the Lord is risen upon thee,' " the Tsar quoted.

There was an exaltation in his voice that was unmis-
takable, and the Duke thought that here was another

example of Russian mysticism and as far as he was concerned he had had enough of it.

"I am glad, Sire, that it brought you so much comfort," he said, finding it difficult to prevent the cynicism from sounding in his voice.

As if she sensed that the Duke walked on dangerous ground, Katharina joined them.

"You are not allowed to talk secrets at my party, Sire," she said gaily to the Tsar, "and I am longing to hear what happened when our English friend called on Princess Ysevolsov."

The Duke looked amused.

He knew that this was Katharina's way of informing him that she was well aware where he had been and that if he thought he could sneak out of the Palace with no-one knowing it, he was much mistaken!

"What did you expect to happen?" he asked.

Katharina looked at him from under her long eyelashes.

"I wondered, for one thing," she said, "whether you met the Ice Maiden and what you thought of her."

"The Ice Maiden?" the Duke questioned.

"Are you referring to Vallon's daughter?" the Tsar enquired. "I was told she had arrived in St. Petersburg."

"She is staying with Princess Ysevolsov, Sire," Katharina answered, "and I am sure she has left many aching hearts behind in Moscow."

"Why is the lady in question called the 'Ice Maiden'?" the Duke asked.

Katharina laughed.

"The Grand Duke Boris can give you a very plausible explanation for that," she replied.

"That is true," the Tsar agreed. "I hear the pavement outside the Vallon house in Moscow is worn thin with his constant pacing up and down."

"But the door is always barred to him," Katharina explained with a little shriek of laughter, "and now that the bird has flown, I am certain that at this moment the Grand Duke is in the depths of despair."

"I find it difficult to follow what you are saying," the Duke remarked in a disagreeable voice.

"It is not really very difficult," Katharina replied. "The Grand Duke is obsessed with Zoia Vallon and has been from the first moment he saw her. But, knowing his reputation, first her mother and then her father barred him from the house, and Boris is not used to being outside in the cold."

"It will do him good!" the Tsar said, then moved away to speak to somebody else.

The Duke thought the same thing. At the same time, he felt unexpectedly angry at the thought of the Grand Duke besmirching anything so pure as Zoia.

For some reason for which he could not account, it had not occurred to him that her beauty would attract men, especially men like the Grand Duke.

She had seemed a creature apart from all the intrigues and machinations of the Social World, which were the same in whatever country he found himself.

But now he began to understand why Pierre Vallon had insisted on his daughter leaving Moscow and coming to St. Petersburg under the chaperonage of Princess Ysevolsov.

She would be well aware, as the Duke was, what kind of person the Grand Duke was—a playboy, promiscuous, always in aggressive pursuit of some woman.

Wherever he went his name was a by-word for notorious love-affairs and extravagant behaviour.

When he was young he had married a dull and unattractive German Princess, whom he left with their children on his country estate and made sure she seldom appeared either in St. Petersburg or in Moscow.

That left him free to stalk like a hungry wolf amongst the lovely women who surrounded the Tsar and who had made the Russian Court one of the most attractive the Duke had ever visited.

It was ridiculous for him, he told himself harshly, to criticise the Grand Duke when his own reputation left much to be desired and his love-affairs were gossipped about in England and had doubtless lost nothing in the telling in St. Petersburg.

At the same time, he could understand Vallon's alarm at the Grand Duke approaching his daughter.

He was quite certain that before she died Princess Natasha had been especially afraid of the consequences of a man with his reputation showing a partiality for a very young girl.

As if she knew where his thoughts were leading him, Katharina said to the Duke:

"Boris is Boris, and we all know exactly what he is like. And after all, the Ice Maiden might do worse for herself."

"Are you suggesting that a girl as young as she is should accept the protection of the Grand Duke, when his reputation stinks to high Heaven?"

The Duke spoke so violently that Katharina looked at him in astonishment.

"I had no idea you had such an animosity against Boris," she said. "Personally, his *affaires de coeur* do not worry me. And for the sake of argument, what alternative is there for the daughter of a French musician?"

"Good heavens!" the Duke exclaimed. "Both you and Sonya Ysevolsov speak as if he were the trombone-player in some sleazy Orchestra! The man is a genius! I have never seen the Prince Regent so moved or so enthusiastic as when he played at Carlton House."

Katharina shrugged her shoulders.

"I grant you his music is good, and he has had a great success in the Music World, but we are talking about his daughter, the Ice Maiden."

"That is what I hope she is where the Grand Duke is concerned!"

"From all I have heard, she indeed offers him no encouragement," Katharina replied, "but perhaps she is secretly in love with some unimportant suitor of whom her father has no knowledge."

The Duke was about to reply that he was quite certain that Zoia would deceive no-one, least of all her father, because it was not in her nature.

Then he thought that by saying so, he would be making a fool of himself over a girl whom he had seen only once and about whom he knew nothing.

What did it matter to him who pursued her, wooed her, or offered her protection?

Even as he argued with himself he knew that everything in him that was decent, every last remnant of his reverence for women, revolted at the thought of anything so spiritual and exquisite being pressured into an immoral association because there was no alternative.

He had an impulse to see Vallon and discuss with him the problem of his daughter's future; to advise him, for instance, to take her to England, where she would doubtless be more readily accepted than in caste-ridden Russia.

There was no snobbery in the world, the Duke thought, greater than that in the Society which centred round the Tsar.

He knew that both Sonya Ysevolsov and Katharina Bagration were right when they said that there was no possible chance of anyone of her mother's breeding offering Zoia marriage.

Yet the Duke found it impossible to think of her stepping down from the pedestal on which he had placed her and becoming soiled and besmirched by the type of life that the Grand Duke was ready to offer her.

'Why should it concern me?' he wondered to himself.

Yet, as he moved about the Reception-Room, meeting old friends and being introduced by Katharina to some of the most important personages in the Tsar's entourage, he knew that he was only giving them half his attention.

In fact, he was not doing his duty of probing deeply into what they were thinking about the war and the consequences of Bonaparte's invasion.

When the Tsar and Tsarina left, the rest of the guests followed, and the Duke realised that if he was to change in time for dinner in the Imperial Apartments, he would have to hurry to his own.

Katharina tightened her fingers on his as he raised her hand to his lips.

"Retire early this evening," she whispered, "for I wish to talk to you."

"Talk?" the Duke queried.

"That is for you to decide," she replied softly.

There was no mistaking the invitation in her eyes or the fire he saw deep down in their dark depths.

"That is what I want," he told himself as he walked away down the long corridor.

Yet, by the time he reached his own bedroom he was thinking not of Katharina but of Zoia.

Once again he was finding it incredible that he should have felt what he had, and not once but twice in her presence experienced what amounted to a vision.

Half-dressed, the Duke moved to the window to look again at the last rays of the setting sun shimmering on the moving water of the Neva.

"It is all the fault of this damned atmosphere!" he told himself, and added as many Russians had done before him: "Why the devil could not Peter the Great have built a city where there was a better climate, in another part of the country?"

He stood staring at the water, thinking what it must be like when it was frozen in winter and the sky and the City of Palaces would seem frozen too.

"The 'Ice Maiden'!"

Would she too melt with the spring that she had made him see when she played him the music that her father had written?

He found himself thinking about the figure that had come towards him through the trees, and then he shied away from admitting who it had been.

He turned round and found that his valet was waiting, holding his evening-coat in his hands.

The Duke shrugged himself into it.

Made by Weston, the tailor patronised by the Prince Regent, it fitted without a wrinkle, and he had already seen the Tsar look at his coats speculatively and with an undoubted touch of envy in his eyes.

The valet added his decorations, taking them from the velvet-lined boxes and fixing them in the correct places on his breast.

The Duke took a quick glance at himself in the mirror, an elaborately gilded one which had come originally from France and was, he knew, unique in both its age and its artistry.

Then as the clock on the mantelpiece warned him that he had only a short time in which to reach the

Tsar's apartments, he set off down the corridors, which seemed to grow longer and longer every time he traversed them.

It was the custom for each Tsar to occupy a different part of the Winter Palace from those inhabited by his predecessors, and Alexander had chosen one that in many ways echoed his taste for simplicity.

The first Romanov to dispense with Royal pomp, he wore no jewellery and refused to allow people to dismount when they met him on the quay.

He liked to wander amongst his guests and had patterned his behaviour on that of an ordinary gentleman, using such phrases as: "I beg to be excused," and, "Please do me the honour . . ."

Unfortunately, in Russian eyes this diminished rather than increased their respect for him.

The Duke was fond of him and always had been because he thought he was trying to rule in a different way from his mad father and the autocratic Empress Catherine.

It was, he knew, no easy task to change anything in the Russian Hierarchy, which in the Palaces ruled far more effectively than did the Tsar himself.

At the same time, the Duke had read the reports from the British Ambassador about the incredible poverty and suffering in Russia, and he knew that in the over-large, flower-perfumed rooms of the Winter Palace he was not seeing the real Russia, which lay outside.

The reports spoke of filthy cellars not far from the Palaces where men and women were huddled together on wooden benches or on bundles of rags on the slimy, wet ground.

There are sixty—eighty—a hundred thousand— who have not enough to eat. There is not a face which is not bleared, blotched, and blurred by drink. Dressed in rags, most of them with bruised faces too sunken to speak, are intent only to stay alive and not be put into the ice-cold ground. They are the dregs of the nation of eighty million and nothing can be done for them, and nobody is in the least interested.

The Duke suddenly felt constrained and stifled.

He could not explain to himself why he had a sudden desire to be free of the Society which he had come from London to seek and which in many ways was more polished and more attractive than he had expected.

"I must get away," he told himself, and was surprised at the urgency of his feelings.

* * *

Tania burst into Zoia's bedroom, where she was sitting mending the lace on one of her gowns, which had been torn.

"Mama is taking me to call on some of her friends," she said. "I asked if you could come, but she wants to take me alone."

"But of course!" Zoia answered. "And I will be here when you return."

"But I wanted you with us," Tania said, pouting. "It is so much more fun when afterwards we can talk over the people we met and what they said."

"If your mother wishes you to go alone with her," Zoia said, "there is nothing you can do about it; but you can store up everything you see and hear and tell me about it, and that will be exciting."

"It is not so exciting for me," Tania complained. "I cannot think why Mama is being so tiresome. She knows how happy we are together."

"Three women without a man to accompany them is an embarrassment to any hostess," Zoia said, smiling. "Go and enjoy yourself, dearest, and when you come back, we will plan a new Ballet-dance to give your mother a surprise."

"I would much rather dance with the handsome English Duke who was here yesterday!" Tania said. "Mama has been talking to me about him, and she says he has a delightful brother he particularly wants me to meet, and that will be something to look forward to when we go to England."

Zoia noticed the word "we" but she said nothing. She only tidied Tania's hair under her high-crowned bonnet, then kissed her gently.

"Do not keep your Mama waiting," she said. "You look very pretty, and I am sure there will be plenty of people to tell you so."

"I do wish you were coming!" Tania said.

She hurried away, leaving the door open behind her.

Zoia rose to close it, then changed her mind and, putting away the lace she had been mending, went downstairs.

Now that there was nobody in the house, it was an opportunity for her to play the piano and try out the new music which had arrived early today from Moscow.

Her father had sent it to her with a letter which told her what a success the Orchestra had been at a performance the previous night, and he had added:

There are rumours, scare-mongers, and a certain amount of quite needless panic. I am glad you are safe in St. Petersburg. At the same time, you will know how much I miss you and how I shall look forward to when we can be together again. Do not

worry about anything but enjoying yourself. I love
you, my dearest daughter, and every time I play
our special music, I know we are very close.

Zoia had read the letter again and again.

There was no-one like her father, she thought, who
could say things which were exactly what one wanted
to hear and which made the heart contract with the
joy of them.

It was true that when they played certain music
they were close in a manner that brought Zoia an
intense happiness.

She felt that it compensated her father a little for the
loss of the wife he had loved with a devotion that had
never wavered since the moment they had run away
together.

'That is the sort of love that I hope to find one
day,' Zoia told herself.

Because she had lived with such an example of
married happiness, she knew that she would never be
content with a love that was not the highest and the
best and which came from a man who was intrinsically
a part of herself as she was a part of him.

It was difficult to put into words what she felt, but
she could say it with music.

Just as many of her father's compositions were written in an effort to express the love he felt for his wife,
so the music she played to herself when she was alone
portrayed her own search for what was beautiful and
holy when it came to an expression of love.

From the moment her father had gone to Moscow
two years ago, there had been men who, having seen
her once, had made every effort to make her acquaintance and court her.

It was then that her mother had explained to her,

in more detail than she had ever done before, her exact position in life.

Zoia had always known that her mother's family, the Strovolskys, were one of the most important in Russia.

Her mother said frankly that she had committed an almost unforgivable crime in running away with the French tutor who had been employed to teach her and her brothers and sister to speak French.

"The aristocratic families here, like those in every other country," the Princess Natasha had said, "do not connect marriage with love, or love with marriage."

Zoia listened wide-eyed as her mother went on:

"I knew that my grandfather was making every effort to find me a husband who would be condescending enough to overlook the fact that my father was only a French musician and accept me as a wife simply because I have Strovolsky blood in my veins."

The Princess's voice sharpened as she said:

"It was not enough! Something within me rebelled at the thought of being condescended to, accepted, as it were, under sufferance."

"I can understand that, Mama."

"I wanted love," the Princess Natasha said softly. "I wanted real love, the love that my mother, rightly or wrongly, had given Count Orlov and which she could never give to any other man."

She put her arm round her daughter.

"One day, my darling, you may have to face the same situation as I did. I promise you that love—real love, such as I have for your father—is worth all the sacrifices that one may have to make for it, and nothing —I repeat, nothing—else is of any consequence."

When Zoia saw the agony her father suffered when her mother died, she knew that while she was watching his crucifixion at losing love, it was still the only thing worth having in the whole world.

She realised too that her mother's death had brought a new dimension to her father's music.

There was a depth in his compositions which had not been there before, and he raised the playing of the Orchestras he conducted to heights that they had never achieved previously.

"That is what love does," Zoia told herself. "It enlarges the capabilities and broadens the horizons of those who find it."

As she went down the stairs now, she heard below her the Princess and Tania leaving the Palace.

She had no intention of telling Tania so, but she understood exactly why the Princess did not wish to take her calling on her friends.

It was not only because she was slightly embarrassed by the fact that Zoia's father was only a musician and a Frenchman at that, it was also because only after they had left Moscow had the Princess realised that despite Tania's beauty she was over-shadowed by her friend.

Doting parents are proverbially blind, and Zoia was sure that when the Princess had extended the generous invitation for her to accompany them to St. Petersburg, she had not expected that she would impinge on Tania's success in the Social World.

Zoia had in fact no wish to go to St. Petersburg and leave her father, but Pierre Vallon had insisted that she do so.

"The Grand Duke is becoming more of a nuisance every day," he said bluntly, "and when I am not with you, my dearest, I worry as to whether he will find some new way of forcing himself upon you. I find that my anxiety interferes not only with my peace of mind but also with my work."

"Perhaps he will ... follow me to ... St. Petersburg," Zoia suggested hesitatingly.

"He may certainly do that," Pierre Vallon agreed, "but the Princess will deal with him more effectively than I can."

Zoia knew what he meant.

It was difficult, even for such a distinguished a man as her father, to stand up to and offend anyone of such importance as the Grand Duke Boris.

But the Princess Ysevolsov could speak to him on equal terms, and Zoia knew that she would certainly not allow him to behave licentiously in any way while she was with Tania.

Because her father was so insistent and because secretly Zoia was rather frightened of the Grand Duke, she had finally agreed to go to St. Petersburg with the Princess and the huge retinue of servants who travelled with them.

They had left Moscow in no less then eighteen carriages, and although the journey had been tiring, Zoia had found herself interested in the country through which they were passing, although sometimes the poverty of the peasants made her want to cry.

The journey had taken quite a long time, for the simple reason that they had stayed with the Princess's friends en route.

It was then that the Princess had realised Zoia's attractions and wished she had not been so hasty in extending her an invitation to stay with them at their Palace in St. Petersburg.

It was the Grand Duke Boris who had christened Zoia the "Ice Maiden," and the name had already preceded her, so that everywhere they stayed, the men in the party eyed her with interest and wondered if perhaps they would be fortunate enough to melt the ice.

The Princess was made furious by their attention.

She wanted everybody to concentrate on her daughter, and although she had already planned that Tania
should make a brilliant marriage, she thought that
learning how to handle men, flattering them and certainly refusing their suit, would be an experience that
should not be missed.

But by the time they reached the second house on
their route, it was obvious that the focus of attention
was not Tania but Zoia, and the Princess made her
plans accordingly.

Zoia, she told herself, should take her rightful place
when they reached St. Petersburg as companion and
teacher to Tania.

There would be no question then of her appearing
in public or accepting invitations to parties.

She did not wish to be unkind, and Sonya Ysevolsov was in fact a warm-hearted woman and made
few enemies.

But she was prepared to fight fiercely and tena-
ciously for the well-being of her child, and she was
determined that Tania should make the most brilliant
marriage any girl had ever achieved.

This, in the Princess's eyes, meant marrying outside
Russia.

She had seen too much of the decadence and licen-
tiousness of the Society under the Romanovs, and it
was impossible to find anybody amongst her husband's relations or contemporaries who was happy.

Even the Tsar, with all his high-flown ideals which
had made so many people think that on his succession
a new era was dawning, had, early in his reign, fallen
deeply in love.

Madame Naryshkina was a dashing Polish lady
who bore him two children and tormented him with
her infidelities.

Because he was so much more of a gentleman than his predecessors, the Tsar took great pains to pay public deference to his wife and they were acclaimed everywhere as the most handsome couple in Europe.

But that was not to say that the Tsar, or for that matter the Tsarina, was happy, and the Princess longed for Tania not only to be of great social importance but to find happiness.

Englishmen, she had always believed, were excellent husbands.

They might have little moments of infidelity, *affaires de coeur* that were conducted with great propriety and discretion, but on the whole they appeared faithful and happy with their wives and their children.

It had therefore seemed providential to the Princess when she learnt that the Duke of Welminster was coming to St. Petersburg as the Tsar's guest.

She herself had not actually had an affair with the Duke, but she had flirted with him and thought him extremely fascinating when they had met both in London and in Vienna.

"He is the type of man I have always admired," the Princess had told herself.

She knew that the Duke found her as attractive as she found him, and it was hard to resist the temptation of taking him as a lover.

But it would in fact be far more of a triumph, she told herself, to have him as a son-in-law, and although he had made it clear that he wished to remain a bachelor, more obstinate men than he had changed their minds on that score.

And while she kept the Duke's brother in reserve, she had not quite given up hope where he himself was concerned.

As they drove away from the Palace she started once again to talk to Tania of the Duke's position in

England, of his magnificent houses and fine possessions, and of the very alluring qualities she found in
him personally.

*　*　*

As it happened, Zoia, as she went downstairs, was
also thinking of the Duke.

She had been conscious of his presence at the back
of the Box while she danced, and she thought afterwards that it was strange that she should notice he was
there.

When she concentrated on her father's music she
was usually carried away completely and so lost in the
world that he created for her that she was oblivious
of everything else.

And yet, somehow, at the back of her mind, hardly
impinging on her consciousness but definitely there,
she had known that there was a man standing at the
back of the Box.

When she made her curtsey she had clearly seen
him behind the Princess, who was apparently unaware of his presence.

Then as she came into the White Salon she had
been aware of him in a manner that seemed still a
part of the music her father had composed.

It was not what she felt about people ordinarily—
it was something different, strange, yet in a way not
strange, only familiar.

It was like a melody to which she listened with her
heart as well as with her mind, and which conjured up
within her the desire to create.

That was what she felt she was doing when she
danced—nothing set, nothing which had been taught
her, merely that which came from within herself.

Her father had understood so well what she felt.

"When I compose, my dearest," he had said, "I

feel sometimes as if I have opened a door within me and let the music come in. Then I only have to listen. It requires no other effort on my part."

"I listen too, Papa," Zoia had said. "Then I know what to do."

They had smiled at each other, knowing that there was no need for words to explain what happened, because they understood.

'The Duke understood too,' Zoia thought as she reached the piano.

She sat down and played a few bars of her father's composition which she had played to him.

Then suddenly, as her father had said, the door within herself opened and she began to play something very different, something she heard, something which flowed through her and into her fingers so that she could translate it into music.

She played, and as she did so, she saw the Duke, his eyes looking into hers, when they had met. Then she saw the expression on his face when she had finished playing to him.

She had known in that second that he had understood what she was trying to convey and had seen what she had seen.

"How is it possible?" she asked.

And yet there was no question that it was possible and that it had happened.

She played on, and suddenly it was no surprise but somehow inevitable that as her music filled the room he should come into it and walk towards her.

She glanced at him and went on playing and he stepped onto the dais and leant on the piano as he had done the day before.

Only after two deep chords, when she lifted her hands from the keys, did the Duke say:

"I knew I should find you here alone."

She looked up at him, her eyes on his.

"How ... did you know ... that?"

"I learnt last night that the Princess and her daughter would call at the Palace this afternoon, and I had a feeling you would not be included."

There seemed to be no answer to this and Zoia was silent.

"I may be wrong," the Duke went on, "but when I came up the stairs and heard what you were playing, I had the strangest feeling that you were thinking of me."

Once again Zoia's eyes were on his, and she said softly:

"I ... was thinking of you ... just as I felt yesterday that when I ... played what Papa had composed, you ... understood."

"I did," the Duke answered. "I fought against it, but I did understand."

There was silence, then he asked:

"Did you compose what you were playing just now?"

"I heard it for the ... first time when I was ... thinking of you."

The Duke drew in his breath.

There was a simplicity in the admission which robbed it of everything but the truth, and yet because it was the truth it was all the more poignant.

"What have you done to me, Zoia?" he asked. "I have never felt like this in my life before."

"L-ike ... what?" she asked beneath her breath.

"Seeing things—hearing things. Being mystic, or any other word you like to call it. It is completely foreign to my nature."

"How can you be ... sure of that?" Zoia asked. "And if it were ... you would not have understood as you did ... understand yesterday."

"Why should it happen?" the Duke enquired almost harshly. "Is it something to do with Russia, or would this have occurred if we had been elsewhere, in London or Paris?"

Zoia looked down at the keyboard before she said:

"I think . . . when things . . . happen to us . . . as you are trying to say . . . it is because we are . . . ready for it. We may hear the same music . . . look at the same picture . . . see the same lovely view . . . and it can mean nothing . . . then suddenly . . ."

Her voice ceased as if she could find no words, and the Duke finished:

"Suddenly there is something else, a vision which I was convinced was only imagination, until I came here today."

Zoia waited and he went on:

"The moment I saw you again I knew it had been real. That is why I am asking—what have you done to me? Why should I feel like this?"

She gave him a smile which he thought was the most beautiful thing he had ever seen.

"It has . . . happened," she said, "and explanations are . . . quite unnecessary."

"But of course," the Duke agreed. "But I am curious. Has this happened with other men?"

There was a sharpness in his voice as if he half-suspected that she was using hypnotism or some other such means of creating an effect.

Having asked the question, he waited, knowing that her reply was of importance out of all proportion to what it should have been.

"Only with Papa," Zoia answered. "He understands . . . he and I feel the same . . . but with . . . no-one else."

The Duke felt himself relax.

He had been afraid of what she might tell him.

"Shall we talk about it?" he asked. "Or will you play to me?"

"Which would you prefer?"

"Both," he said with a smile.

He leant against the piano while Zoia lifted her hands, then looked down at them and unexpectedly dropped them back into her lap.

"Y-you are . . . making me . . . shy," she said. "I . . . I cannot . . . think of the . . . music . . . because you are here."

"In other words, you are thinking of me," the Duke said in his deep voice.

"You . . . you want me to . . . play to you."

"Let it wait," he said. "Come and sit down on the sofa and tell me about yourself."

He straightened himself, ready to move away from the piano.

For a moment Zoia did not rise.

"I think Her . . . Highness would be annoyed if she knew you . . . came here when she was . . . out," she said slowly, as if she had just thought of it, "and we are . . . alone."

"Does it matter?" the Duke asked. "Perhaps she will not know."

"She will know," Zoia answered, "because the servants will tell her. Everything is . . . known in Russia.

That was true, the Duke thought, just as Katharina had known yesterday that he had left the Palace to visit the Princess.

He told himself that it was not important and he did not care what she said or thought.

Then he remembered that it concerned Zoia too, and for the first time he realised that in his desire to see her again he had been incredibly selfish.

The Duke was so used to thinking only of his own

interests, his own pleasures, that he never considered how they affected other people.

For the first time in many years, he found himself concerned with the effect of his actions on another human being, and most especially on the girl facing him.

"I suppose the correct thing for me to do would be to leave at once," he said.

He looked at her and went on:

"I want to stay—God knows I want to stay! There is so much I want to talk to you about, so much I want you to tell me. But in case it should hurt you in any way, in case there should be any unfortunate repercussions, I will give you a message for the Princess and leave."

Zoia clasped her hands together, and it was an instinctive little gesture which made the Duke draw in his breath.

"I want you to ... stay," she said in a very low voice. "I should so much like to ... talk to you ... but I suppose it would be ... right for me to ask you ... to go."

"Let us compromise," the Duke suggested quickly. "I will stay a little longer, but we must not waste one second of our time together."

He put out his hand over the piano towards her.

"Come," he said. "Let us sit down comfortably and make the most of being alone."

She rose, and as she did so, she put her hand in his.

As they touched each other, they were both aware of the vibrations that passed between them, inescapable and compelling.

They had been about to step down from the dais, but now neither of them moved. Zoia only raised her eyes and looked into the Duke's, and for a moment time stood still.

"That is what I might have expected," he said.

His voice broke the spell.

She took her hand from his and walked across the room to sit on the satin-covered sofa which stood between the marble pillars.

He found himself watching the grace with which she moved and thinking that it was almost as if she floated rather than walked and there was music in every movement.

He sat down beside her, turning so as to look at her, his eyes searching her face.

"I heard a great deal about you last night," he said when she did not speak. "They tell me you are called the Ice Maiden."

Her eyes dropped a little shyly and a faint touch of colour came into her cheeks.

"It is . . . a foolish name," she said, "thought up by a . . . foolish person."

"Why should you say that?" the Duke asked.

"Because I am not really . . . enclosed in ice," she answered, "except to one . . . particular person."

"The Grand Duke!"

"Yes . . . I do not like him . . . and he attempts to . . . threaten Papa."

"In what way?" the Duke asked sharply.

"He told Papa that he would have him driven out of Russia, that he would not be allowed to conduct here unless . . . unless I did as he . . . wished."

"That is intolerable!" the Duke said angrily. "The Grand Duke has no right to behave in such an uncivilised manner."

"That is what . . . Papa said," Zoia replied, "and he told the Grand Duke he had no jurisdiction over him. At the same time . . . I am afraid."

"Why?"

"The Grand Duke is a very obstinate and determined man. I have a feeling that he could also be . . . wicked and . . . unscrupulous if it suited him."

"You will be safe here in St. Petersburg."

"I . . . hope so," Zoia answered. "Her Highness is . . . very kind."

"I am sure she will protect you, at any rate," the Duke said, "and if you are in any trouble, I am here also."

Zoia looked at him and he had the feeling that she looked deep into his heart as if she was searching for something. Then she said quietly:

"You must not be . . . involved in anything which might make . . . trouble for you with the Tsar. I have heard how . . . fond he is of you . . . and Russian affairs should not concern you . . . personally."

The Duke smiled and answered:

"But you are not Russian—not entirely. You are half-French."

"That makes it worse!" Zoia said. "England is at war with France!"

"So is Russia at the moment," the Duke said.

"I am worried about Papa in Moscow. If the French reach it, the fighting will be . . . terrible."

"I feel sure that the Russians will do everything in their power to prevent the French from getting as far as Moscow," the Duke said slowly.

"It is all so . . . horrible . . . so unnecessary," Zoia said. "I loved Paris when I was a little girl and we lived there . . . and it breaks Papa's heart to think of all the men who have been killed quite senselessly and for no reason except the insatiable ambition of a man who is not even French . . . but Corsican!"

It was a cry, the Duke thought, that he had heard

so many Frenchmen make, and he had no answer to it. Instead he said:

"I know I shall involve you in a lot of difficulties if I stay here any longer, but I will see you again, and if you are really in any trouble, do not hesitate to let me know."

He paused, then added:

"Promise me you will do so."

"I . . . promise," Zoia said softly.

He thought it was typical of her that she did not prevaricate, did not try to dramatise what he had said as so many other women might have done.

They both rose and the Duke took Zoia's hand in his.

She felt his lips on the softness of her skin.

"Take care of yourself," he said quietly, then left the room without looking back.

She stood for a moment staring after him.

Then, as if she would still the tumult within her, her hands went to her breasts.

Chapter Four

Princess Ysevolsov and Tania called first on an ancient member of the Ysevolsov family who lived in a fabulous Palace on the bank of the Neva.

She was so old and had lived through so many dramatic events in her life that she was not particularly interested in what was happening at the moment.

She was, however, a tremendous admirer of the Tsar and talked incessantly of his charm and his commanding appearance.

She had recently been visited by *Madame* de Staël, the French writer who had extolled him to all and sundry, saying that she was deeply affected by the noble simplicity with which he entered upon the great interests of Europe.

"Alexander," the old lady went on, "is exactly the type of Tsar that the Russians have wanted for many centuries, and you will see that history will give him the place which he deserves."

Tania found the visit rather boring but contented herself with admiring the many attractive objets d'art with which the Palace was decorated.

When they left, her mother said:

"At least one person is satisfied with the way in which Russia is being ruled, but I cannot help feeling that such praise of His Imperial Majesty is exceptional."

"I think everybody admires the Tsar, Mama," Tania answered. "He is so handsome and looks so commanding in his uniform."

The Princess bit back the rather bitter words which came to her lips and instead started to talk once again of the Duke.

"You must show him every attention, Tania," she said. "Smile at him, ask his opinions, but above all things, do not bore him with commonplace observations."

"What are they, Mama?"

The Princess, looking at her daughter, admitted to herself that while Tania was exceedingly lovely, her brains were not likely to entertain such a sophisticated man as the Duke.

Their next call was at the Winter Palace, where they enquired if it was possible to have an audience with the Tsarina.

Elisabeth Feodorovna had always been extremely fond of the Princess, and it was not surprising when the message came back that she would be delighted to see her.

The Princess and Tania were led to her private apartments, and here again Tania was beguiled by all the attractive little ornaments with which the private rooms were decorated.

The Tsarina, however, was talking very seriously to the Princess.

She was, owing to the crisis, happier with the Tsar than she had been for some time.

He no longer frittered away the hours with Maria

Naryshkina. Instead, he looked for the support of his wife, which she gave him whole-heartedly.

The Princess thought that the Tsarina remained magnificently resolute.

"You are very courageous, Ma'am," she said.

"I try to be," the Tsarina replied simply; "but how can I tell you of my inner emotions when my dear and well-beloved Russia, for whom I feel at this hour as for a darling child, is wretchedly sick?"

She gave a deep sigh and went on:

"I am certain that God will not abandon her, but she will suffer, and I with her, sharing every spasm of her anguish."

The Princess put out her hand to press the Tsarina's and make her understand how much she sympathised in her suffering.

Then in a quiet voice the Tsarina went on to talk of her fund for war-orphans and how she herself had handed over to charities nine-tenths of her annual allowance.

It was growing late in the afternoon and the Princess was thinking that the Tsarina would indicate that their interview was at an end, when the door burst open and one of the Ladies-in-Waiting came rushing in with a distraught look on her face.

"Your Majesty—Ma'am!" she cried.

The Empress rose to her feet, an apprehensive expression on her face as she asked:

"What is wrong? What has happened?"

"They are saying, Ma'am," the Lady-in-Waiting answered almost incoherently, "that the French are starting a diversion in the direction of St. Petersburg."

"It cannot be true!" the Tsarina exclaimed.

"I was told this by the Captain of the Golden Guard, Ma'am, who had been informed that the Government are planning the evacuation of valuables."

"I do not believe it!" the Tsarina cried. "I must go to His Imperial Majesty at once!"

She went from the room and the Princess, taking Tania by the hand, started to make her way to the entrance of the Palace.

The corridors were already full of people running hither and thither, talking at the tops of their voices and yet saying little that made any sense.

There were Chevalier Guards in their gilt breast-plates—Bishops wearing the white *klobouk,* or high white veils falling from the crowns of their hats to their shoulders—and Court Arabs who were actually gigantic Negroes in *skorohods.*

The Princess bumped into a friend, who cried:

"It is intolerable, inconceivable that we should be threatened here! Surely someone will stop the enemy before they can reach us?"

"I am sure that is what will happen," the Princess said soothingly.

"I swear I would tear out my tongue rather than speak the French language again!" her friend cried hysterically. "And every French man and woman in St. Petersburg should be expelled from the city immediately, or sent to Siberia!"

She spat out the words venomously, then seemed to be swept away down the corridor by other people, running, shouting, and screaming out vehemently against the French and their leader, Napoleon.

The Princess found her carriage waiting, and as she and Tania drove away, the girl said tentatively:

"Will the French kill us, Mama?"

"I am sure that your father and the Russian Army will stop them long before they reach St. Petersburg," the Princess said firmly.

At the same time, she crossed herself as she spoke and murmured a prayer beneath her breath.

Back at the Ysevolsov Palace, everything seemed to be calm and quiet after the tumult of the Winter Palace.

It was obvious that the news had not reached the servants, and the Major Domo merely stepped forward to say:

"His Grace the Duke of Welminster called when you were out, Your Highness."

The Princess frowned.

"Did you tell him at what time I would return?"

"He did not ask me, Your Highness, but he spoke for some time with *M'mselle* Vallon, and she may have conveyed the information to him."

"He spoke with *Mademoiselle* Vallon?" the Princess asked sharply.

"He asked for her, Your Highness, and I informed His Grace that she was in the Music-Room."

The Princess's lips tightened.

She had thought several times of the strange manner in which the Duke and Zoia had stood staring at each other when they first met.

It had seemed peculiar at the time, and now, as she remembered how interested the Duke had seemed in Zoia, her eyes darkened.

Without saying anything to Tania, she swept up the stairs, and before she reached the landing she heard the sounds of music which told her where Zoia was to be found.

She opened the door.

Zoia was sitting at the piano, her face raised, her eyes lifted as if she was looking into space and was unaware of what was happening in the world round her.

She had a radiant expression which made her look more lovely than the Princess had ever seen her before.

Sharply she banged the door behind her, shutting out Tania, who had followed her mother upstairs.

The sound jerked Zoia back to reality.

She ceased playing and rose slowly to her feet as the Princess advanced towards her.

When she reached the piano, the Princess said sharply:

"I understand the Duke of Welminster has been here."

"Yes, Ma'am."

"And he stayed for some time?"

"Not for very long, Ma'am."

"How long?"

"I do not know exactly," Zoia replied.

"You know as well as I do that you have no right to entertain gentlemen in my absence. It is not the way I expect a young woman staying in my house to behave."

"I am sorry, Ma'am," Zoia answered, "but the Duke came into the room unexpectedly. When he realised you were not at home, he talked for a few minutes, then left."

"What did he say? What did he talk about?"

Zoia was quiet for a moment, then she answered:

"About music . . . and my father."

Because she appeared to answer the question in such a straight-forward and truthful way, the Princess should have been placated, but somehow it seemed to make her angrier than she was already.

All the resentment she felt at Zoia over-shadowing Tania, the manner in which she attracted men without apparently making any effort, seemed to boil up inside her until she could no longer contain herself.

"Your countrymen are marching on St. Petersburg," she said. "They threaten our lives and everything we hold dear and sacred. You had best return to your father, for I have no intention of sheltering an enemy!"

As the Princess spoke, Zoia's eyes widened and there was no doubt of her astonishment at what she heard.

Then as the Princess finished, almost spitting the last words at her, Zoia said quietly but with a dignity that was unassailable:

"I understand, Ma'am, and I will leave immediately for Moscow. I can only thank you for your hospitality and say that my father and I are very grateful."

She curtseyed, and the Princess, as if she was suddenly aware of how young and slight Zoia was, said in a voice that was a little less aggressive:

"I will order a travelling-carriage for you and enough of our most-trusted servants to accompany you and ensure your safety."

"Thank you, Ma'am."

Zoia curtseyed again and went from the room.

* * *

The Duke was with the Tsar when the rumour that Napoleon was now moving towards St. Petersburg was brought to him. Alexander read the despatch and his face paled as he handed it to the Duke without saying a word.

The Duke read the sprawling, half-unintelligible writing on the communiqué and said:

"Quite frankly, I do not believe this, Sire."

"Why not?" the Tsar enquired.

"Because if it was true, you would have heard from General Kutuzov himself."

"The despatch is not from him?"

"No, Sire. It was sent to you by Count Povolsk, who I think you will remember was in your Suite when we met in Vienna."

"Yes, yes, I remember," the Tsar said.

"I always thought the Count to be a dilettante and a gossipper. I do not know what position he holds in the Russian Army, but I would not rate it very high."

The Tsar snatched the despatch from the Duke's hand and read it again.

"I believe you are right," he said. "We should not pay too much attention to this until we have further confirmation from Kutuzov himself."

Unfortunately, when the Duke left the Tsar's apartments he found that the despatch had been read by members of the Government before it reached the Tsar, and the Courier who had carried it had conveyed its contents to everybody he had met.

It was the kind of thing, he knew, which would never have happened in the British Army, and he was appalled at the hysteria which had taken possession not only of the Palace but of the inhabitants of St. Petersburg.

He soon learnt that the majority of the noble families were packing their valuables into carriages and moving from the city to their houses in the country.

Only the poor would be left helpless and unprotected, and crowds of them now stood outside the Winter Palace, staring at the huge edifice as if they felt that only some Divine Providence linked with the Tsar himself could save them.

The Duke was sure that with Moscow directly in their line of advance and far nearer, it was extremely unlikely that Napoleon would change direction and march on St. Petersburg.

What he might do after capturing Moscow was a very different thing, but the Duke, who at one time had been a soldier himself, was quite certain that from a Military point of view St. Petersburg was not the immediate objective.

It was, however, difficult to find anyone to discuss it with him, let alone agree.

Finally he talked to Lord Cathcart, the British Ambassador, who informed him of something which he had not known before—that Sir Robert Wilson, who was known as "the English General," was with the Russian Army.

Sir Robert had acquired in Europe a reputation as an expert on Russia at war when he had written a book published two years earlier and studied by all the Military specialists of the age, including Bonaparte himself.

Lord Cathcart informed the Duke that Sir Robert had been sent by the British Government from Turkey to the Russian Front and had arrived only just in time to witness the fall of Smolensk.

"He is with them now," Lord Cathcart said, "and I am in fact awaiting a report from him about what is occurring."

He smiled as he added:

"You will understand, Your Grace, that I find his reports very much more credible than those which come from the Russians and often mislead the Tsar."

The Duke settled himself more comfortably in the chair in the Ambassador's very impressive Reception-Room.

"I am very relieved at what you tell me, My Lord," he said, "and if it is true that you are expecting a despatch at any moment, I would like to wait for it."

"I shall be delighted for you to do so," Lord Cathcart replied.

However, the Courier carrying the despatch from Sir Robert Wilson did not arrive until very late in the evening.

The Duke stayed on at the British Embassy for dinner, and only when they had finished an excellent meal did a servant intimate to the Ambassador that the Courier had arrived.

There was no doubt that both the Ambassador and the Duke were tense as the former undid the despatch.

The Ambassador read it first; then, with a sigh that was obviously one of relief, he passed it to the Duke.

Robert Wilson wrote crisply and positively that he understood that General Kutuzov intended to halt his retreating troops, who had been moving steadily backwards from the advancing French, and would engage the invaders in battle before they reached Moscow.

"That is Bonaparte's objective," he wrote. *"And there is no doubt that he must be prevented from achieving it."*

That was the end of the despatch, which was a short one, and the Duke looked at the Ambassador with a smile as he said:

"I was certain that the panic that has swept St. Petersburg was unnecessary."

"So was I," Lord Cathcart agreed.

He rose to his feet.

"I must carry this immediately to the Tsar," he said, "but I would be grateful, Your Grace, if you would be kind enough to inform any members of the Government who are available of what we have just learnt."

"I will do that," the Duke agreed.

It was, as it happened, no easy task. However, nearly three hours later the Duke knew that he and the Ambassador between them had got a great number of panic-stricken orders countermanded and had prevented a number of people of importance from leaving the city.

By that time the Duke was very tired, and when finally he retired to his bedroom he hoped that Katharina would not demand his attention.

He had not really had time during the day to think of what his reaction last night had been when she had come to him as before through the secret panel in the wall.

He had known as she advanced towards him, wearing a new and even more attractive negligé than she had worn the night before, that his interest in her had died and, incredible though it seemed, she no longer attracted him.

He had not for one moment assumed that their interest in each other was anything but a passionate exchange between two sophisticated people who appreciated the expertise of making love.

That physically she was eminently desirable went without saying, and the Duke without conceit knew that she did not exaggerate when she described him as an exceptional lover.

She amused and aroused him.

What was more, his knowledge that she was there to spy on him gave a piquancy to their affair which he appreciated as she did.

Then, quite unexpectedly, almost like a bomb-shell, he knew that his feelings for her had changed, and even if he had wished to do so he could no longer play the role of lover.

Because he was half-prepared for his reaction to what she expected of him, he had not undressed.

His valet had taken away his evening-coat with its decorations, and he had loosened his tightly tied cravat, but when she appeared he was still wearing his fine lawn shirt and black satin knee-breeches with the diamond garter glittering against his black silk stockings.

Before Katharina could speak, before she could ask the obvious question as to why he was not in bed, the Duke said quickly:

"I have some urgent despatches to write, Katharina, and they will keep me busy until the early hours of the morning."

She smiled.

"Then I will write them with you. You know I wish to read them."

"Unfortunately, they will be in code, and although your countrymen have attempted to break it, I do not think as yet they have managed to do so."

"That is true," Katharina said, "and all the more reason, my adorable Blake, for you to translate them to me."

"Can you imagine my committing such treachery?" the Duke asked. "I have not asked you to show me your confidential reports."

"You may see them if you wish," Katharina replied, "but I can tell you far more easily what I think about you, and what you are like as a—man."

The last word was a caress in the way she said it, and the Duke answered quickly:

"Go to bed, Katharina, and leave me with my work."

"Can you really be so unkind?" she asked.

She moved towards him, and before he could avoid it her arms were round him and her lips were against his shoulder.

He could feel them warm and possessive through his thin shirt, but as she touched him he knew, as he had known when she came into the room, that she no longer had any power over him.

It was difficult for him to believe it because their liaison had been so fiery, their desire for each other almost a violent confrontation.

The Duke put his fingers under Katharina's small chin and turned her face up to his.

For a long moment he looked into her eyes, seeing

the fire lurking in their depths while her breath was coming quickly through her parted lips.

'How has this happened?' he wondered to himself, and knew the answer as if somebody had said it aloud.

Only when Katharina had left him reluctantly and he was alone as he wished to be did he walk to the window and pull back the curtains to breathe in the hot, windless air.

As he did so, he heard in his mind the music which Zoia had played and which her father had called "The Melting of the Ice."

As he listened, he thought to himself that it had melted within him years of cynicism, of assuring himself that women fell into only two categories: those who were desirable and those who were not.

Tonight it was not a physical barrier that had been erected between himself and Katharina but an idealistic one.

He felt as if he were a Knight entering a joust, and because he carried the favour of his lady, all other women had ceased to have any meaning for him.

It seemed utterly incredible, and yet he knew it had happened.

The music that Zoia had played seemed to deepen and to encompass not only his mind but a strange part of his anatomy which he had not known for a very long time but which he had once called his soul.

* * *

When the Duke rose the following morning he found that the Palace had returned to normal and the confusion and chaos of the day before might never have happened.

The Grenadiers of the Golden Guard were as impassive as statues as the Duke proceeded along the corridors to the Tsar's apartments, and the people he met, who were mostly Officials, walked slowly and circumspectly, passing him with a respectful bow as though they had never heard of the word "panic."

The Tsar was in an excellent mood, certain from his Bible readings of the night before that Kutuzov would, because he was favoured by God Himself, prevent the French Army from reaching Moscow.

As the Duke listened to him, an idea gradually began to present itself to his mind, but for the moment he did not voice it.

However, he left the Palace as soon as he could excuse himself from attendance on the Tsar, and set off once again in the direction of the Ysevolsov Palace.

He told himself that it would be only polite to let Princess Ysevolsov of all people know that the rumours, which she would undoubtedly have heard, of Napoleon marching in the direction of St. Petersburg were untrue.

But he knew that his real motive for going to the Ysevolsov Palace was to see Zoia again.

All last night, when without bothering to write any despatches he had got into bed, he first thought of her, then dreamt of her.

"She is beginning to haunt me," he told himself, and wondered once again if it was part of the mystery and the climate of Russia—or did the explanation lie in something he would not yet admit to himself?

At the Ysevolsov Palace he was pleased to see that there were no carriages being loaded in the courtyard, and when he asked for the Princess he was taken immediately to her private Sitting-Room.

As he was announced, the Princess, who was sitting at her *secretaire,* writing, gave a cry of delight and rose to her feet.

"Blake!" she exclaimed. "I am so delighted to see

you, and I am sure you can answer many questions which I am longing to ask."

"I expect you have already heard," the Duke replied, "that the panic yesterday was only a rumour spread by that indefatigable scandal-monger Count Povolsky.

The Princess laughed.

"I might have guessed that Felix would be at the bottom of it, but fortunately one of my friends called late last night to say that he had seen Lord Cathcart and there was no need for any of us to get excited."

"I felt that you, if nobody else, would be sensible," the Duke said.

"I must order you some refreshment," the Princess said smiling. "Will you have coffee or wine?"

"Coffee, please," the Duke replied.

The Princess rang a gold bell and gave the order.

The Duke waited until the door shut behind the servant, then he said:

"I hope that Zoia Vallon was not upset by the rumour. I feel sure she is already deeply concerned with the fate of her father in Moscow."

"Pierre Vallon is a Frenchman," the Princess said coldly, "and after what we all felt last night, it will take some time before any of us regard the French as anything but our most implacable enemy!"

The Duke looked at her in surprise.

"Surely that does not include Vallon and his daughter?"

"I am afraid," the Princess said, "that when my husband is likely to be killed by a French bullet and his country invaded in this despicable manner, I have little use for French citizens whoever they may be!"

The Duke was astonished, but because his concern was instantly for Zoia, he said quickly:

"May I speak to Vallon's daughter? I feel she must be extremely distressed by your attitude."

"There is no reason for you to concern yourself," the Princess replied. "After all, she is nothing to you."

"I was extremely struck by her talent as a dancer," the Duke replied, "and also by the way she plays the piano."

He mentioned the latter deliberately, knowing full well that the servants would have told the Princess that he had been to the Music-Room while she was playing.

"That I can well believe," the Princess answered, "but I suggest we talk of other things, for I have no intention, dear Blake, of quarrelling with you over an unimportant young girl who was merely teaching my daughter French."

"We certainly will not quarrel," the Duke answered, "but I would still like to speak to Zoia. I feel sure you will not prevent me from doing that."

He saw the Princess's eyes narrow for a moment. Then she said:

"So persistent? I must say, Blake, I am surprised at you. I never thought for a moment that a young girl would really interest you, but if so, why not my little Tania?"

"I have already said that I think Tania would suit my brother admirably," the Duke replied patiently. "I will also, and this is a promise, give a Ball for her at Welminster House when you bring her to London."

The Princess was well aware what a concession this was, and she clasped her hands together as she said:

"That is wonderful of you, Blake, and I know exactly what it will mean for Tania as an *entrée* to the *Beau Monde*."

She gave a little laugh and put her fingers to her lips.

"There, you see, I am speaking French when everybody swore yesterday that never again would a French word pass their lips! But how else could one describe the glittering, exclusive circle in which you are such a prominent figure?"

"You are very flattering, Sonya," the Duke said, "but I still wish to speak to Zoia."

The Princess's eyes met his and he thought she intended to defy him. Then with a smile that had something slightly spiteful about it she said:

"Unfortunately, that is impossible."

"Why?"

"Because Zoia left at dawn this morning for Moscow!"

"You mean you sent her away?"

"I sent her back to her father."

"Why?"

"Because she is French and I thought she would be safer there when feelings here against the French were running so high."

"You really thought that Moscow, which at any moment will be within reach of Napoleon's guns, is safer?"

The Duke spoke scathingly, and the Princess looked at him a little apprehensively before she said:

"It is none of your business, Blake, what I do in my own household or with someone who is more or less a superior servant."

The Duke rose to his feet.

"You are leaving?" the Princess asked, and now there was a note of consternation in her voice.

"I am leaving," the Duke replied. "Good-bye, Sonya."

He raised her hand perfunctorily to his lips, bowed, and left the room.

"Blake!" she called in a pleading tone just before

the door closed behind him, but he appeared not to hear her.

The Duke returned to the Palace, gave orders to his valet to pack his things immediately, then went to the Tsar's apartments.

Alexander was engaged with a number of Statesmen, but as soon as he was free the Duke was admitted to his presence.

"What is it, Welminster?" he asked. "I have a feeling that you would not have asked to see me urgently unless it was important."

"It is important to me, Sire," the Duke replied. "I have decided that after the commotion and confusion of last night, I should, in the interests of my own country and perhaps of yours, go immediately to try to make contact with Sir Robert Wilson."

"You would liaise with my Army?"

"I should like to have the pleasure of meeting General Kutuzov," the Duke replied, "and to be able to see for myself exactly what is taking place. I think that after last night, Sire, we would both of us be rather sceptical of despatches, from whichever direction they come."

"The Government behaved with quite unseemly haste," the Tsar said sharply. "I have already spoken to them sternly, telling them that in the future they must make sure of their facts."

"You are right to do so, Sire," the Duke agreed, "and if you will not think it an impertinence, I should like to send you my own observations on what is occurring when I am in touch with Kutuzov."

"Please do that," the Tsar said. "You know I trust you, Welminster, and I shall always be grateful for your help yesterday evening."

There was no need for the Tsar to express in words that he was ashamed that he, his Government, and a large number of other Russians had panicked with very little reason for it.

Leaving the Imperial Apartments, the Duke hurried to his own and found as he expected that everything was ready for him to leave immediately.

He wrote a hurried note to the British Ambassador, and because he felt it was the decent thing to do, he wrote one also to Katharina.

Then, almost like a boy hurrying to go home from School for the holidays, he ran down the marble staircase and out to where a *drotski* was waiting for him, with another for his valet, and six mounted soldiers ordered by the Tsar to be his escort.

As they drove away from the Palace the Duke felt as if he was setting out on a voyage of discovery.

Not only as far as the war between the two Armies was concerned, but as regarded himself, his feelings, and perhaps, although he was not sure, his whole future.

* * *

The Ysevolsov travelling-carriage, drawn by four horses, was very swift, and Zoia already knew that Prince Ysevolsov, like so many other nobles, had his own horses stabled at convenient stopping-places between St. Petersburg and Moscow.

She thought that at the rate they were travelling she would be with her father within five to six days and knew that in some ways it would be a great relief to be with him.

Yet he might be angry with her for coming into danger which included not only the threat of the French but also that of the Grand Duke Boris.

He had made life intolerable for her until her father had persuaded her to leave Moscow.

Because the Grand Duke could not obtain entrance

to the house to see her, he stayed permanently outside the door, preventing her from going out and making his presence known by a long stream of presents,
bouquets of flowers, and letters.

She refused to communicate with him and his gifts
of any value were returned immediately by the servants.

But it had given her the uncomfortable feeling of
being besieged, and she was always frightened that
the Grand Duke, in his frustration, might take his revenge upon her father.

No Russian, whoever he might be, would dare to
defy or offend anyone as important as the Grand Duke.

But while Pierre Vallon laughed at his threats and
discounted his rudeness, Zoia trembled, knowing the
obstinacy and determination in the Russian character
which would make a man fight and go on fighting even
after he was beaten.

That was what Zoia prayed Bonaparte would find
as he invaded Russia, but so far he had been victorious and the Russians had been defeated in every en-
gagement.

She could not help feeling that her sympathies
should be torn in two between the conflicting forces,
since she was half-French and half-Russian.

But she told herself that in this instance, if in none
other, her sympathy was entirely with the land of her
mother.

The French had no right, she thought, to invade a
country which had done them no harm and in fact
for a short time had been their ally.

She had learnt that the Tsar had sent a message to
Bonaparte at Vilna, saying that it was not too late to
maintain peace even now, if the Emperor would take
his Army back across the Niemen.

"Even God could not now undo what has been started," Napoleon had answered.

Zoia had been told that when Alexander received the reply he remarked:

"At least now Europe will know that we are not beginning this slaughter."

But whoever began or ended it, men on each side would die, and to Zoia there was something terrible in thinking of the young men who would not only be shattered by the guns but also be wounded and left to ebb out their lives in agony because there was no-one to attend to them.

"War is wrong and wicked!" she had often said to herself passionately, and she found herself praying that no-one she loved would either be killed or wounded.

And somehow her prayer inevitably included the Duke.

She had known when he left her that he took some part of herself with him.

She had wanted him to stay, wanted when she turned again to the piano to see him and to hear his voice, to feel that strange vibration between them that seemed to strike into her very soul and somehow make her his captive.

Now they had been parted and she felt, as the horses carried her away on the road to Moscow, that they would never meet again and probably he would soon forget her very existence.

It was an inexpressible agony within her heart, and at the same time she could not imagine it possible that this could have happened.

He had walked into her life so unexpectedly, and yet in that second when their eyes met she had felt as if she had found him after centuries of time.

She dared not attempt to understand what had happened to her. She knew only that it had, and suddenly the music which she heard within herself and which she could express with her fingers had a new meaning.

Even her prayers had changed, and when she thought of the Duke her whole being seemed to come alive.

But she was leaving him, leaving him behind in St. Petersburg, and perhaps he would never know why she had left. Perhaps it would be days before he even knew she had gone.

Because this hurt her, she felt as if her whole being winged through the ever-widening space between them to reach him.

And yet, she asked herself, how could she think for one moment that she could ever be of any importance in the Duke's life, though already he meant so much to her?

She now understood exactly what her mother had said to her when she had explained why she had run away with Pierre Vallon in spite of the importance of her position in her grandfather's household, the grandeur in which they lived, and the distinction of being a Strovolsky.

It was all of no consequence beside love.

But, Zoia thought, her mother's position was very different from her own.

Her mother had loved a man who was considered to be her inferior, while she loved a man who was infinitely her superior in every way. He was a man of great distinction, and of different nationality, so that between them lay a gulf as wide as the distance from the earth to the moon.

"I must forget him!" Zoia whispered to herself, and knew that it would be impossible.

She would never forget him, and she thought that because of what she had felt for him on the three brief occasions when they had met and he had filled her whole world, perhaps she would in fact always be the Ice Maiden, as they declared her to be.

On and on the horses travelled.

They stopped for picnic-meals which the servants had brought with them and for a change of horses.

They travelled both by day and by night because it would have been impossible for Zoia to stay alone at night in an Inn.

What was more, she had always been told that they were scruffy, dirty, and lice-ridden, and doubtless at the moment they would be filled with the Military.

So that those who escorted her could get some sleep, they often stopped for an hour or so by the road-side, and the men who drove the carriage and rode as outriders merely dropped down on the ground, warm from the great heat of the sun, and slept soundly.

Then they would awaken refreshed and ready to ride on.

It was constricting, but Zoia grew used to the movement of the carriage beneath her, and sometimes she felt as though she were on a pilgrimage to which there was no end, and the rumble of the wheels seemed to fill her ears to the exclusion even of thought.

Then, when they were coming towards what she thought must be the end of their journey, there was the distant sound of gun-fire.

She had seen the movement of Russian troops in increasing numbers and one of the servants had told her that the peasants had said that the Russians were preparing to counter-attack.

Zoia wondered where this would be. The night before, when they had stopped for a meal beneath some trees, she had asked the coachman where they were and he had pointed to the south and said: "Borodino."

She had known, for she had heard of it before, that it was not far from Moscow, and she thought with relief how wonderful it would be to see her father tomorrow or the day after.

She only hoped that he had not, by some frightening mischance, left the city and she would find herself alone there without him.

But his letters had seemed so calm, so unperturbed, that she could not believe that he would run away, and certainly he would not move unless his Orchestra went with him.

Now, as dawn broke and they started on their way, she heard again cannon, far away to the south, and knew that the battle everybody in St. Petersburg had been waiting for had begun.

Zoia felt almost as if she was being threatened by those on each side of the conflict, the Russians because she was French and the French because she was Russian.

She found herself praying for her own safety, and somehow she found herself praying for the Duke's safety as well, although why he should be in any danger she had no idea, for she was sure that he was in St. Petersburg.

On and on the horses travelled and now at last there were the domes and spires of Moscow ahead.

"I am home!" Zoia told herself, for home was where her father was, although it could never be the same since her mother was no longer there.

She was tired, for it had been a long journey, and as she still heard the noise of cannon, now far away in the distance, she thought that the men facing the firing must be tired too, although by now many of those on both sides would be dead.

She shivered at the thought, thinking once again

that it was a cruel waste of the most precious gift God had given mankind—the gift of life.

Now they were in Moscow and she saw that the streets were filled with people, all obviously tense and waiting for the outcome of the battle.

The carriage drove along the riverside and past the Kremlin with its high pointed towers, and then, some way farther on, they turned up a street where there were well-built stone houses.

Her mother had always said that she had no wish to live in a house built of wood, and because Pierre Vallon had loved his wife so much that he had always been prepared to do anything that would make her happy, he had bought a house in a quiet Square some way from the centre of the city, and Natasha Vallon had been delighted with it.

"There is a garden where Zoia and I can sit under the trees," she said, "and where, when it is warm enough, you and I, darling, will have our breakfast. It is like an adorable doll's-house and we will be very happy here."

Pierre Vallon kissed his wife.

"You have never grown up," he said. "A doll's-house is what I should give you in every country where we have to live."

His wife looked at him in an adoring fashion.

"As long as it is a home to which you will always return," she said softly, "I would be happy in a garret or a cellar. It is of no consequence to me."

He put his arms round her, and Zoia, who was watching, knew that he was moved by her mother's words in the same way that music moved him, so that there was a look in his eyes which she could only describe to herself as one of rapture.

The Doll's-House, as they teasingly called it, had been a little oasis of peace and happiness where Pierre

Vallon could escape from everything—even from his admirers who pursued him relentlessly.

It was only the Grand Duke Boris who had upset the peace and quiet, and Zoia had been more thankful than ever for the garden when she dared not leave through her own front door for fear of encountering him.

Now for the moment there was no fear that the Grand Duke was lurking outside, and as the carriage drew to a standstill she jumped out of it before her attendants even had time to knock on the door.

It was opened by her father's Housekeeper, who stared at her in surprise.

"*M'mselle* Zoia!" she exclaimed.

"I am back, Maria!" Zoia answered. "Is Papa here?"

"He's in the garden, *M'mselle,*" Maria replied, and Zoia sped through the house.

Her father was sitting in the shade of a tree, with sheets of music in front of him, and she knew that he was writing down his latest composition for his Orchestra to play.

She paused and stood for a moment looking at him.

Could any man, she asked herself, be more handsome or more attractive?

Then her heart answered: "Yes, there is one," before with a little cry which startled Pierre Vallon she ran beneath the branches of the trees.

"Papa! Papa! I am home!"

She saw the surprise in her father's eyes, and then his arms went round her and he was holding her close.

"Zoia, my dearest! Why are you back? How could you do anything so crazy as to return at this dreadful moment?"

Chapter Five

"The troops are abandoning the city, Sir," Jacques said as he served Zoia and her father luncheon.

"Nearly everybody else seems to have left already," Pierre Vallon replied.

Zoia looked at him in surprise and he explained:

"The Governor has forbidden the people to leave, pleaded with them, and brought back and punished those he could catch, but they still continue to slip away with their carriages full of everything they can pack into them."

"But I am sure the Russian Army has stopped the French," Zoia said. "I heard the guns in the distance soon after dawn. It must have been about six o'clock. I cannot bear to think of how many men must have been killed."

"One cannot have war without casualties," Pierre Vallon replied. "I can only pray that the battle was decisive, one way or another."

Even though he spoke as if it mattered little to him which side won, Zoia was quite certain that in his heart he knew that his own countrymen were the aggressors.

Napoleon had acquired so much already, she thought. Why should he want more? Why should he wish to master Russia as well as nearly the whole of Europe?

"There's a new broad-sheet, Sir," Jacques said, bringing it from the side-table on which he had put it.

"What does it say?" Pierre Vallon asked, without attempting to take it from him.

"It declares that General Kutuzov will defend Moscow to the last drop of his blood!"

"That is what I suppose he is doing at this moment," Pierre Vallon remarked.

As he spoke, he was obviously listening and Zoia could also hear very faintly, for they were a long distance away, the thundering of the cannon.

It seemed to her, although it was difficult to tell if it was a fact, that the firing was more intense, more explosive than when she had been on the road approaching the city.

"We are safe ... here?" she asked, and there was just a tremor of fear in her voice.

"I imagine we will be safe, whichever side is victorious," her father replied drily. "But I wish, my dearest, that you had stayed in St. Petersburg."

Because she thought it would hurt him, Zoia had not told her father that the Princess had literally turned her out.

Instead she said:

"If there is danger, I want to be with you, and I know that is where Mama would wish me to be."

Her father smiled at her and she saw the sadness in his eyes which was always there when he thought of his wife.

He rose from the table and walked to the window to look into the sunlit garden.

"What we have to decide," he said, "is if it is best for us to stay or to leave."

"If we leave, where shall we go?" Zoia asked.

"That, of course, is the problem," he replied. "What do you think, Jacques?"

There was nothing unusual in Pierre Vallon discussing his plans with the man who was ostensibly their servant, for actually his position was a very different one.

Jacques had been an unsuccessful actor who had met Pierre Vallon by chance and had dedicated his life to his service.

He had had a very unhappy childhood. He had wandered about in Circuses, taking part in minor turns, and although he had been given small parts on the stage, no-one had been interested in him or wished to retain his services.

Then, by chance, when he was out of work he went to the Opera and saw Pierre Vallon conduct.

From that moment, as he had told Zoia, he found his soul and knew that this was what he had been searching for all his life.

He had now been in their household for nearly ten years, and it was difficult to imagine what life would be without him.

Apart from anything else, Jacques had an aptitude for languages and he not only spoke German because he had lived in Vienna and Arabic because he had visited Egypt, but now he was surprisingly proficient in Russian.

He could act the part he wished to play much more convincingly than he was able to do on the stage, and Zoia knew that whoever occupied Moscow, Jacques would be able to converse with them and prove that he was a kindred spirit.

"I suppose it will be difficult to get food if the shopkeepers have left and the shops are closed," she said aloud.

"I've got in a good store, *M'mselle*," Jacques answered.

She smiled because she knew that whoever else went hungry, her father would not, if Jacques had anything to do with it.

"One thing I must insist upon," Pierre Vallon said with a note of authority in his voice which Zoia had not heard before, "you are not, for any reason whatsoever, to leave the house."

"Do you mean that, Papa?" she asked, remembering how frustrated she had felt before she left Moscow because the Grand Duke's behaviour had forced her to remain a prisoner.

"I mean it!" Pierre Vallon said firmly.

He looked at Jacques as he spoke, and the two men were thinking that an almost empty city would be a temptation to the Russian soldiers, let alone the French who had fought their way for so many weary miles from their homeland.

Looting was always one of the "perks" of war, and both men were certain that there would be uncontrollable looting, just as a woman—any woman—would be a temptation to men separated from their wives or sweethearts.

"You are to stay in the house," Pierre Vallon repeated, and as if he did not wish to say any more, he went from the room.

"You were unwise to come back, *M'mselle*," Jacques said to Zoia. "It'll worry the Master, and he doesn't work so well when he is worried."

Zoia glanced over her shoulder at the closed door before she answered:

"I had to come, Jacques, only do not tell Papa. People in St. Petersburg thought that Napoleon might be marching in that direction and suddenly everybody hated the French and the Princess wished to be rid of me."

Jacques shrugged his shoulders.

"C'est la guerre, M'mselle, and in war anything may happen."

As her father had done, Zoia went to the window.

She thought that she could hear the thunder of the cannon although it was really too far away, and she could imagine the sound of the falling shells, the moans and cries of the wounded, and the smell of blood and powder.

She had never seen a battle and yet she instinctively felt the horror of it, and she turned away from the sunshine and moved into the small Salon at the front of the house.

Then suddenly at four o'clock in the afternoon she sensed a silence, and she knew without being told that the battle was over.

Now it was the question of who had won.

Zoia had a feeling of apprehension which was different from anything she had felt all day, and she did not understand why she was so tense and in a way afraid.

She ran from the Salon in search of Jacques, and when she found him polishing a piece of silver in the kitchen, she said:

"I know the guns have ceased! The battle is over! Oh, Jacques, please find out what has happened."

"The Master should be home soon," Jacques replied.

"He will be with the Orchestra," Zoia answered, "and I cannot wait until he returns. Please, Jacques, find out if anybody knows the result of the battle."

"I don't like leaving the house with only two women in it," he said, "but to please you, *M'mselle,* I'll see what I can learn. Bolt the door after I've gone, and don't open it to anyone except the Master or myself!"

"No . . . of course not," Zoia agreed.

At the same time, it made her feel strange to hear such instructions from Jacques.

She went to talk to Maria, but it was hard to keep her mind on anything but the battle and her anxiety to know what had occurred.

It was nearly two hours before Jacques returned. As soon as she heard the knock on the door, Zoia ran down the stairs, peeped through a side-window, and saw him outside.

She pulled back the bolts and turned the key, and he came into the small Hall.

He was smiling and she knew before he spoke that he had good news.

"What has happened? What have you learnt?"

Her words seemed to fall over themselves.

"They say it's a great victory, *M'mselle.*"

"For the Russians?"

"Of course! They always said that General Kutuzov would stop Napoleon from reaching Moscow."

"Then we need not worry any more," Zoia said in delight, and ran upstairs to tell Maria the good news.

When her father came back he did not seem as pleased and excited as she had thought he would be.

"There have been terrible casualties," he said. "Some of the wounded are being brought into the city and there is practically nobody still here to attend to them."

"Surely not everyone has gone, Papa!" Zoia cried.

"There are only the poor and the homeless to be seen in the streets," Pierre Vallon replied. "And do you know how many of my Orchestra came to the rehearsal I called for this afternoon?"

"How many?" Zoia asked.

"Six!" he replied.

He flung the music-sheets he held in his hand down on the table as he said:

"The Orchestra is finished! I am no longer wanted!"

"Oh . . . Papa!"

Because Zoia felt the pain in his voice, she went towards him and put her arms round him.

"You will always be wanted," she said reassuringly, "if not in Russia then in a dozen other countries. You know that!"

"They were coming along so well," Pierre Vallon said almost beneath his breath. "I felt that because they were your mother's countrymen, they somehow kept me in touch with her."

He spoke more to himself than to his daughter, and Zoia pressed her cheek against his and said:

"Wherever you are, I know Mama is always with you. You were too close ever to lose each other."

She felt her father's arms tighten round her and knew that that was what he wanted to hear. Then as if he could not bear to talk any more, he went to the room that was his special sanctum and shut the door behind him.

Zoia went to find Jacques.

"I think, Jacques, that it is time for us to leave Russia," she said, "and for Papa to build up another Orchestra somewhere else."

"I agree with you, *M'mselle*," Jacques replied. "What we have to decide is where to go, and we must persuade your father to leave."

"It will not be easy," Zoia agreed, "but I will talk to him about it after dinner this evening."

"You do that, *M'mselle*, and I'll cook him a very special dinner—all the dishes he really enjoys!"

Jacques was a superb cook and Pierre Vallon, like every other Frenchman, enjoyed his food.

That would set the scene, Zoia knew, and all she had to do was to try to convince her father that his talents would be more appreciated somewhere else. Then they would be off on their travels again.

Even as she thought of it, she found herself wishing that she could see the Duke just once more.

She wondered if he knew that she had left St. Petersburg. Perhaps he had come back to ask her to play to him again and learnt that she had gone.

Without even shutting her eyes she could see his handsome face, his steel-grey eyes, and the expression which was almost one of bewilderment as he asked her what had happened to him—why he had felt as he had.

"He understood Papa's music," Zoia said beneath her breath, as if she reassured herself that it was true.

The memory of the moment when their hands had touched and something magnetic, something inexplicable, had passed between them was unforgettable.

Slowly she walked up the stairs, and because it was to be a very special dinner for her father and she had a feeling that it was an important one, she was deciding which of her gowns she would wear.

Her father always liked her to be well dressed, as he had wanted her mother to be.

He had a Frenchman's appreciation for a woman who was elegant as well as beautiful, and when she reached her bedroom Zoia went to her wardrobe, opened it, and looked at the gowns which hung there.

There were none of the gowns she had worn in St. Petersburg because as they had been creased through being packed, Maria had taken them to another room where she would press them before putting them in Zoia's wardrobe.

But there were several lovely gowns which she had

left behind, and amongst them was one which she knew was her father's favourite.

"I will wear that one," she told herself, and could not help wondering whether the Duke, if he saw her in it, would think it attractive.

Then she almost laughed at the idea that he would notice anything she wore.

It had been obvious from the things the Princess had said that beautiful women fluttered round him not only in St. Petersburg but especially in London, where he was of great social importance.

Zoia felt her spirits drop.

'He will never think of me again,' she thought. 'Why should he?'

And because it was so painful to think of her own insignificance, the sunshine seemed to have lost its brightness.

* * *

It was nearly four hours later and Zoia was ready for dinner, which Jacques had said would be late because he had so much cooking to do.

She was putting the last touches to her hair when she heard a loud knocking on the front door.

It startled her and instantly the thought of the Grand Duke Boris sprang to her mind.

It was the manner in which his servants, as arrogant and imperious as their Master, had knocked day after day, often hour after hour, when she was in Moscow before.

"Surely he cannot have learnt that I am here already?" she asked herself.

Then she thought that it was extremely unlikely that the Grand Duke had remained in Moscow when all the other noble families had left.

The knocking came again and now Zoia rose from

the stool in front of her dressing-table and went to the top of the stairs.

Below her she saw Jacques struggling into his uniform-coat and pulling off the white apron in which he had been cooking, then hurrying across the Hall to the front door.

He opened it, and Zoia heard him speaking in Russian to someone outside.

She could not hear what was said even though she learnt over the bannister, then Jacques turned from the door and, looking up as if he had suspected that she would be there, cried:

"*M'mselle,* please come here at once!"

*   *   *

The Duke, travelling in a carriage drawn by six horses with a small troop of soldiers to escort him, drove towards Moscow at tremendous speed.

Like Prince Ysevolsov and all the other nobles, the Tsar stabled his horses along the road between St. Petersburg and Moscow, but His Imperial Majesty's were at closer intervals than those of his subjects.

This meant that with a frequent change of horses the Duke was able to complete his journey in far less time than anyone else.

He recalled that once the Empress Catherine had reached Moscow in three days, but for her the horses were changed every hour.

The Duke was a good traveller, and the swaying of the carriage, which many people found disagreeable, did not perturb him.

He had slept some of the time, and for the rest he had sat thinking a great deal about Zoia—in fact, she continually impinged on his thoughts even when he wished to concentrate on the situation that he would find when he reached Borodino.

Actually, when he arrived it was a few minutes after four o'clock, and the overwhelming noise of guns, which he had heard during the last hour of his journey, had ceased.

He was, however, well aware that a tremendous battle had taken place, for as he drew nearer he could see, to the south of the road on which he travelled, the fearful spectacle of a battlefield disappearing into a far horizon and apparently covered with dead and wounded soldiers.

It was so horrifying that he found it difficult to believe that he was not seeing a vision rather than the actual truth of what had occurred.

When he alighted from his carriage he saw a number of Staff Officers gathered on an incline above the road, below which were tens of thousands of men lying dead in various attitudes, while amongst them wounded soldiers with scared faces were struggling to move away from their fallen comrades.

Fortunately, the Duke found General Kutuzov with the Officers and immediately made himself known to him.

Kutuzov was speaking quietly and without elation in his voice, but there was no doubt that he was convinced that he had achieved a notable victory.

The Duke waited while the General finished dictating a despatch to the Tsar and gave it to a young Officer who was waiting to carry it to St. Petersburg.

The Duke knew only too well that it would be received there with peals of bells from the Churches, fireworks, and chains of lanterns along the banks of the Neva, and every vessel in the port would be illuminated and be-flagged.

He was certain that Kutuzov would be rewarded with a Princely title, a huge sum in roubles, and doubtless a Marshal's baton.

He also thought, with an inexpressible relief, that now Zoia would be safe in Moscow, and if he did not spend too long with the Generals he would have a chance of seeing her tonight.

He liked the idea of being the person to inform her and her father that they and their home were safe.

He therefore congratulated General Kutuzov and his Staff, then went in search of Sir Robert Wilson.

He was not far away and was obviously pleased to see the Duke.

"I was told that you were in St. Petersburg, Your Grace," he said, "and I wondered how soon I should see you at the Front."

"It is obvious that I have arrived too late to be of any help," the Duke replied with a smile.

Sir Robert, however, looked grave.

"I hope that General Kutuzov is not sending despatches to the Tsar claiming an overwhelming victory!"

"That is exactly what he has done," the Duke replied.

He saw the frown between Sir Robert's eyes and asked:

"Are you telling me that such an assumption is premature?"

"I believe so."

"Why?"

"Because the cost of the battle is inconceivable."

The Duke looked grave.

"What have you lost?" he asked.

"It is absolutely impossible at the moment to calculate the number of men killed," Sir Robert replied, "but at a conservative estimate, the Russian Army must have lost forty thousand men."

"Impossible!" the Duke said with a gasp.

"I may be wrong—I hope to God I am!" Sir Robert said. "But you only have to look at the battlefield to see the devastation in front of you, and the guns have been firing since six o'clock this morning."

"That would be ten hours," the Duke calculated.

"Exactly!" Sir Robert agreed.

"And what are the French losses?"

"That we do not know," Sir Robert replied. "They will be heavy too—very heavy!"

It was obvious that Sir Robert had no more to tell him, and the Duke went back to the road where his carriage was waiting amongst a melee of soldiers being regrouped, wounded men being lifted onto stretchers, and horses being employed to move guns.

The Duke was just going to step into his carriage and tell the coachman to drive on to Moscow when he saw another vehicle approaching and recognised the livery of the coachman on the box.

As the four horses drew nearer he knew that he was not mistaken—it was Prince Ysevolsov's carriage, and he was sure that it was the one which had carried Zoia to Moscow.

He walked down the road towards it and, putting up his hand, caused the coachman to draw the horses to a standstill.

The footman on the box recognised him and jumped down, and another man riding with the escort did the same thing.

The servants greeted him respectfully and the Duke asked:

"You have taken Miss Zoia Vallon to her father's house in Moscow, I think?"

"That is right, Your Excellency."

"Will you give me the address?" the Duke asked.

The man was about to reply when two horses pulling a gun forced them to move aside to let it pass.

There were several soldiers in charge of it, all giving orders at the same time, and the Duke could see that they were covered with dust and dirt and were tired to the point of exhaustion.

The wheels became stuck in the ground, and before the horses could proceed, an Officer came up to demand:

"What are you doing? Where are you going with that gun?"

"We were told to move it, Sir," one of the soldiers answered, "because there's a shell stuck in the barrel and it can't be fired."

"What do you mean it can't be fired?" the Officer demanded aggressively.

"It's stuck, Sir."

"Then fire it! We cannot have the guns moved from their positions, in case the French attack us again."

Looking at the sea of dead bodies between the Russians' present position and that of the French on the horizon, the Duke thought that this was unlikely, but the Officer, fussily authoritative, said:

"Fire the gun now! Fire it in the direction of the enemy. If it kills a few more of those damned invaders, all the better!"

One of the men obediently forced a ram-rod down the barrel of the gun, saying as he did so:

"We've tried this a dozen times, Sir. The shell won't budge."

"Then try it again!" the Officer snapped.

They obeyed him.

There was an explosion, and to the Duke, watching, the whole world seemed to burst into flames. . . .

* * *

Zoia reached the front door and saw standing outside on the steps two of the servants who had brought her to Moscow.

She was surprised to see them, thinking that they would already be on their journey home.

However, she smiled at them and said:

"Good-evening! Is anything wrong?"

"It's just that we didn't know what else to do with His Excellency, *M'mselle,*" the elder of the two men said in broken French.

Zoia did not understand, and Jacques explained:

"They say, *M'mselle,* that the gentleman was telling them he was coming to see you when a gun accidentally exploded. Three soldiers were killed, one of His Highness's servants and his horse, and the gentleman's valet. The gentleman himself is badly wounded."

Zoia felt as if her heart was constricted and it was hard to breathe.

"What gentleman?" she asked, but she knew the answer.

She ran down the steps and across the pavement.

She saw that the side of the carriage had been badly damaged by fragments from the explosion, and as the door was opened she looked inside to see the Duke lying on the back seat, covered with blood.

"His Highness's house here in Moscow is closed and everyone has left," one of the servants said in an apologetic tone. "We didn't know where else to take him."

"You were right to bring him here," Zoia said.

Turning to Jacques, she said:

"Tell them to move him carefully—very carefully."

It was not until the men had carried the Duke upstairs and laid him on the bed in the only unoccupied bedroom in the small house that Zoia, looking frantically at Maria, asked:

"He is . . . not dead?"

It was not surprising that she should ask the question, for the Duke's face was devoid of all colour, his eyes were closed, his whole body was limp, and it appeared as if he had no life left in him.

"He's not dead yet, *M'mselle,* and if it's God's will, we'll keep him alive," Maria answered briskly.

She immediately took charge in the practical manner of a Frenchwoman confronted with a situation which was not hopeless as long as there was something that could be done.

Prince Ysevolsov's servants were told to find a Doctor. Jacques gave them several addresses in case the Doctors as well as everybody else had left Moscow.

Zoia was sent to the kitchen to boil water while Maria and Jacques undressed the Duke to ascertain the extent of his wounds.

When Zoia came upstairs with the kettle, a basin, and a number of linen towels, the Duke was between the sheets and she thought he was looking even paler and more lifeless than he had before.

Now her father was there, and his calm acceptance of the situation was more comforting than anything he might have said.

"A Doctor should be here soon," he said as if Zoia had asked the question. "They will not all have left Moscow—in fact I know that the wounded are being taken to the empty houses of those who have run away."

Even as he spoke there was a knock on the door.

* * *

It was after eleven o'clock when Zoia and her father sat down in the Dining-Room to a somewhat inadequate meal. They had not thought of eating while there was so much to do for the Duke.

"You met His Grace in St. Petersburg?" Pierre Vallon asked.

"Yes, he came to visit the Princess when Tania and I were dancing in the little Theatre."

Pierre Vallon looked at his daughter, and they were too close for him not to realise that the tone in which she spoke merely confirmed the impression he had gained when he had seen her looking at the Duke upstairs.

"You mean something to each other?" he asked quietly.

"It was ... very strange, Papa, but the moment I met ... him, I knew he was ... different from any man I had ever met before."

"In what way?"

"For one thing, he understood your music, and when I played to him ... he ... saw what we had ... seen."

There was no need to say any more. Pierre Vallon understood so much that was not expressed in words.

"You are sure?" he asked.

"Quite, quite sure, Papa. You know I would not be mistaken about anything like that. Besides, the next day when he called and found me alone, he asked me what I had ... done to him. He said he had never felt like ... that in his ... whole life."

"It is extraordinary!" Pierre Vallon murmured.

"That he should feel like that?"

"That the Duke of Welminster should," her father replied. "I met His Grace while I was in London and again in Vienna. From all I have heard about him, and people talk about him quite a lot, I should not have imagined for one moment that he would be as you say he is."

Zoia smiled.

"You know I could never be mistaken Papa, and no-one . . . no-one but you, has ever . . . understood before."

Pierre Vallon did not answer for a moment, then he said:

"You know, my dear, that I would never doubt anything you tell me or interfere unnecessarily with any friendship you might make, but if your mother were alive I feel sure that she would explain to you that the Duke of Welminster can mean nothing in your life."

"I have . . . thought of that, Papa."

"It would be best," Pierre Vallon said slowly, "if tomorrow I arrange for His Grace to be moved to a Hospital. There must be one where he can have every attention, perhaps better than we can give him here."

Zoia was silent for a moment. Then she said:

"In a way, Papa, I feel responsible for what happened. His Highness's servants said that the Duke was asking for my address when the gun exploded."

Her father did not reply, but she was well aware that he was thinking that the Duke had no right to intrude on their private life, no right to pursue a girl who did not belong to the Social World.

Zoia gave up pretending to eat and clasped her hands together.

"When you fell in love with Mama," she said in a low voice, "did you have any . . . choice as to whether you . . . loved her or whether you did . . . not?"

Pierre Vallon looked at his daughter and there was no mistaking the consternation in his expression.

"Are you telling me that you love this man?"

"Yes . . . Papa."

"But how can you be sure? You have seen him twice, perhaps three times."

Zoia smiled and it seemed to illuminate her face.

"Really, Papa!" she said. "How can you, of all people, ask that question and expect me to answer it?"

"In my case it was different," Pierre Vallon said.

"Was it?" Zoia queried. "Mama said that from the moment she saw you she fell in love with you and she thought that you loved her too."

"How could I help it?" Pierre Vallon asked. "She was so lovely, so exquisite in every way. And, my dearest, you are very like her."

"Not only in my features and my eyes," Zoia said, "although I have your fair hair, but in the ... things I ... feel."

She gave a little laugh that seemed to ring out so spontaneously that her father found himself smiling too.

"How can you expect me to be anything but your daughter?" she asked. "I see what you see when you play, hear what you hear, and try to express myself in music as you do. But I am also Mama's child."

Her voice softened as she went on:

"As you know, Papa, my heart has never been touched until this moment. That is why the Grand Duke and quite a number of other people call me the Ice Maiden. But from the moment I ... looked into the Duke of Welminster's eyes, from the ... moment I touched his hand, the ice ... melted, and I was in love!"

"Do you understand that there can be no happy ending to this story?" Pierre Vallon asked.

His voice was filled with pain, as if he hated to know how much she would suffer.

"I am aware of that," Zoia replied. "But it still does not prevent me from loving him, even though I am sure he will never love me in the same way."

"I will arrange for him to go to a Hospital."

"No, Papa."

"In this you must be guided by me," he said. "I do not wish to hurt you. You know I want only your happiness, but for him to stay here is madness, and I cannot contemplate where that madness would end."

Zoia knew that he was saying without words that what the Duke would offer her would not be marriage.

She gave a deep sigh.

"I know that you are thinking of me, Papa," she said quietly, "but every instinct in my body tells me to look after the Duke and nurse him back to health."

"And every instinct in mine tells me to protect you," Pierre Vallon retorted, "to keep you from making yourself eventually much more unhappy than you will be if you say good-bye to him now. Think of what has occurred as a dream, a fantasy that has brought you something beautiful, just as music will bring you the same thing."

He paused for a moment before he went on:

"If you do not see the Duke, if we leave him here in Moscow as I intend to do, then gradually the feelings he has evoked in you, the image of him that you have in your mind, will vanish."

He made a gesture with his hands as he said:

"Of course, the music you have played for him will bring it back, and you will always have a certain nostalgia for the moment in your life when you first fell in love, but there will be other loves, other moments —that I promise you!"

"How can you be sure?" Zoia asked. "If, when you left Prince Strovolsky's Palace, Mama had not gone with you, would you have forgotten her?"

She knew as she saw her father's face that he wanted to lie but was unable to do so.

"Was your love for Mama really different from what I feel for the Duke?" Zoia asked, pressing home her point.

Her father did not answer and she went on:

"You have taught me, Papa, to analyse my own feelings. You have also taught me to distinguish what is real and true from what is false, and I know that what I feel now is not the adolescent romancing in which I sometimes indulged years ago. This is as real as breathing, hearing, and seeing!"

She gave a little sigh as she said:

"If the Duke never spoke to me again, and if as you suggest I never saw him again, I should still love him, and I am absolutely certain in my own mind that I shall never feel this way for anybody else."

There was a silence which seemed full of a thousand unspoken words. Then Pierre Vallon said:

"I do not know what to say to you, my dearest."

"Then shall we leave things alone for the moment and just nurse the Duke back to health? Then we will face the fact that I must go out of his life, and I expect eventually he will want to go out of mine."

"I would still like to look for a Hospital," Pierre Vallon said. "I promise I will do nothing without consulting you first, but I have a feeling that the Duke may be ill for longer than I wish to stay in Moscow!"

"You intend to leave so quickly?"

"I want to go," Pierre Vallon replied. "After the slaughter there must have been today on the battlefield, I shall feel uncomfortably self-conscious of being French."

It was not only that, Zoia thought to herself, because his nationality had never worried him before. It was because he was bitterly disappointed and hurt that his Orchestra had left without telling him, had deserted, it seemed in the very moment of victory.

She could understand how in their hour of fear they had wanted to take their wives and children out of the city which might be invaded by the French.

They would now return, she told herself, and if they apologised to her father he would forgive them, for he was the type of person who could never bear a grudge for long.

At the same time, she knew how deeply he would feel if he had been abandoned by those who had trusted him, and she thought that perhaps even they had said to themselves:

"After all, he is only a Frenchman. Why should we trouble about him?"

Dinner was finished, and Zoia, without making any excuse, went up the stairs to see the Duke.

Maria was with him and when Zoia appeared in the doorway she left the room and came out into the passage.

"How is he?" Zoia asked.

"It's difficult to tell, *M'mselle*. The Doctor is coming again tomorrow and hopes to bring with him someone who is more experienced in such injuries than he is. That is, if there is anyone left in Moscow."

"Did the Doctor say that?"

"He said that people have been leaving every day and every hour, and, apart from anything else, it's impossible to get supplies for the wounded."

"I cannot understand how they can be such cowards!" Zoia said indignantly.

Maria put out her hand consolingly.

"Don't worry, *M'mselle*. We'll look after the gentleman one way or another. He's a strong man, and that will count in his favour more than anything else."

Zoia's eyes searched the older woman's face.

"Are you telling me that his life is really in danger?"

For a moment Maria hesitated, then she told the truth.

"He's bad, *M'mselle,* but not so bad that we cannot save him with careful nursing."

She saw Zoia's face and added quickly:

"Now don't you go upsetting yourself. He'll run a high fever, there's no doubt about that, and there's nothing you can do about it. But Jacques and I will look after him. You can trust us."

"You must let me help too," Zoia said quickly. "I may not be as experienced as you, Maria, but I know that I can help him. I know that I can give him some of my own strength."

She did not wait for Maria's reply, but passed her and went into the bedroom.

The Duke was lying very still, and again Zoia thought, with a constriction of her heart, that he might be dead.

Then she reached out her hand and touched his, and there was still some warmth in it.

To see him so quiet, so lifeless, was like seeing a great oak-tree fallen to the ground.

Then with both her hands holding his, she felt as if she poured the life-force from her own body into his.

She could feel her spirit reaching out to his spirit, and at the same time she knew that her heart was searching for his heart and offering him her love.

"O, God, make him well and strong again," she prayed. "He must live. Do not take life from him . . . but let him live."

It was a prayer that came from the very depths of her being, a prayer that strained every nerve and every feeling within her.

Then she said aloud to the Duke:

"I love you . . . think of me . . . come to me . . . I am yours . . . and I want you . . . alive."

There was, of course, no response from the Duke.

But she felt that in some way which she could not interpret, in whatever darkness and oblivion he lay, she had enveloped him in her love and could somehow reach him.

Chapter Six

"The smell of burning is worse!"

The Duke spoke in a low voice, and at the first sound Zoia rose from the arm-chair in which she had been sitting and went to his bedside to say:

"I thought you were asleep."

He looked up at her, thinking that her hair, silhouetted against the light from the windows, formed a halo round her head. Then he said:

"You are not answering my question. The smell is worse than it was before."

"I think the wooden houses in the ... next street are on fire," Zoia replied.

"I have already said that you and your father must leave Moscow at once," the Duke said. "I am sure the Doctor can find somewhere for me to go, and I must not keep you here any longer."

He spoke with an effort but his tone was firm.

Zoia smiled.

"Do you think we could ... desert you or hand you over as a ... prisoner to the French?"

"It has to be done," the Duke said. "When the

Doctor comes again, I will ask him to find somewhere for me."

Zoia did not reply for a moment.

She was thinking of the twenty-five thousand wounded Russian soldiers who had been brought into Moscow after the battle.

The Government had instantly said that there was no proper accommodation for them in the city, and because they could not be attended to they were to be sent away to other towns.

Once the order had been given, it was found that there were no vehicles in which to evacuate them, and although some had got away, ten thousand Russians remained in Moscow before the French brought in their own wounded.

Even now it was difficult for Zoia or anyone else to believe that Moscow, the Holy City of Russia, had been evacuated without a shot being fired in its defence.

The French had arrived to find the place practically deserted.

Pierre Vallon had been told that Napoleon was stunned by the emptiness of the streets and the abandoned houses and shops.

Only the very poorest and the aged who had no means of transport had remained, and they had crowded into the Churches for safety.

After the French had moved in, the soldiers, completely out of control, began looting and, because there was plenty of wine, soon became hopelessly drunk.

Fires had broken out amongst the wooden houses but no-one knew if they had been deliberate actions on the part of the Russians or whether they were accidental.

Zoia had learnt from Jacques that large parts of the city were already in ruins and the conflagration was worse because when the Russians had left they took the fire-engines and hoses with them.

At night, when everything was quiet, Zoia standing at her open window could hear in the distance the rumbling of falling walls and the excited shouts of the soldiers.

In the day-time there was no escaping from the smell of the smoke or the sight of it, thick and black, rising above the roofs.

She knew that her father was afraid of what would happen to them, and the reports that Jacques brought back from the center of the city where the French were encamped were more and more depressing and discouraging.

"I must get you away," Pierre Vallon said not once but a hundred times to his daughter.

"How could we leave the Duke, Papa, even if it were possible for us to escape?" Zoia would ask.

Last night when they had the same conversation, Pierre Vallon had risen from the table at which they had been sitting to say sharply:

"Pack everything which is of vital necessity."

Zoia had looked at him apprehensively.

"What do you intend to do, Papa?"

"I intend to get you away before the house is burnt over our heads," he said, "or, worse still, the soldiers break down the door in search of loot."

Zoia heard the fear in his voice and knew that he was afraid not for himself but for her.

Quietly she answered:

"I will go with you, Papa, but we must take the Duke with us."

Her father did not reply.

This morning when he left the house, he had kissed her and said:

"Keep the door securely locked, and you and Maria

be ready to leave at the first possible opportunity. I am taking Jacques with me to make arrangements."

"With whom, Papa?" Zoia had asked, but he had not answered her.

She had locked the door behind him. It was now the back door they used, for Jacques had boarded up the front door of the house so that it looked as if it were unoccupied.

Jacques had said that the looting soldiers were usually in such a drunken state that they did not trouble to force their way into any building that was difficult, preferring houses like those of the nobles which had simply been abandoned with full cellars.

It seemed incredible, after all General Kutuzov had said about defending Moscow to the last drop of his blood, that he should have withdrawn his Army and left the road clear for Napoleon and the French to march into the ancient city.

But the enormous number of casualties which the Russians had suffered had made it impossible for Kutuzov to attack the French or even to defend the city.

When the Duke had recovered consciousness and was well enough to understand what had occurred, he realised that Sir Robert Wilson had been nearly right in what he had anticipated the casualties would be.

Forty-three thousand Russians had been killed or wounded, and thirty thousand French.

The report of the great victory which General Kutuzov had despatched so quickly to the Tsar was a hollow triumph when Moscow had to be abandoned.

Pierre Vallon, perhaps because he was French, realised what a desperate disappointment to Napoleon his entry into the hallowed Capital had been.

There had been for him almost a mystic significance in the thought of finding the five hundred domes, gilded or painted in brilliant colours, waiting for him, only to discover a week later that he was in fact in possession of a heap of smouldering ruins.

"What will the Emperor do now, Papa?" Zoia had asked.

"I am sure he expects that the Tsar will ask for an Armistice."

Zoia had repeated this conversation to the Duke, and after thinking over what she had told him, he had said:

"I believe that the loss of Moscow will have a traumatic effect on the Tsar and on the Russian people."

"What do you mean by that?" Zoia had enquired.

"I have a feeling," he said, "that the yawning gap between the nobles and the peasants will be closed— at least for the time being—and the Tsar, fortified by the deep religious fervour which possesses him at the moment, will refuse to negotiate."

"What makes you so sure that will happen?" Zoia asked.

He looked at her with his grey eyes and said quietly:

"Ever since I have known you, I have felt as if I have a 'sixth sense' that I have never used before."

She gave a little sigh.

"I knew you had that when you . . . listened to me playing and you . . . understood what Papa had meant when he wrote the music."

"I do not understand myself," the Duke said reflectively.

Then he closed his eyes as if he was too weak to go on with the conversation.

For the first three days after being brought to Pierre Vallon's house he had been desperately ill and had run, as Maria had expected, a very high fever.

She and Jacques had sponged him down regularly with vinegar, and although she had not admitted it to Zoia, at times Maria had thought that there was nothing they could do to save his life.

But he had survived, and the Doctor ascribed it to his being so fit.

"A very strong young man!" he had said with satisfaction.

Zoia, however, believed that it was the life-force which she had poured into him whenever they were alone.

"You must get well," she said to him in her soft voice while he lay unconscious. "You are wanted in the world. There is so much for you to do. Come back! Come back from wherever you are!"

She felt as if her spirit called on his spirit, and as every day he grew stronger, she was sure that she sustained and strengthened him in a manner which would be laughed at by Medical Science.

Now he was better, but still very weak, and she wondered, although she did not say so aloud, whether a long journey would be too much for him, even provided that her father could get him away.

She knew how fanatically Napoleon loathed the English, who had frustrated him at every turn.

It would be inconceivable to leave the Duke a prisoner in French hands.

He was apparently asleep when she heard the knock on the back door which told her that her father and Jacques had returned.

Quietly she left the bedroom and sped down the stairs, and found when she reached the kitchen that Maria had already let in the two men.

Because every time Pierre Vallon left the house there was always the fear that he might not return,

Zoia ran towards him to put her arms round his neck and kiss his cheek as he said:

"I have good news!"

"What is it, Papa?"

"I have obtained from the Emperor himself not only a permit to leave the city but the promise that we shall have an escort until we are outside the walls."

Zoia did not speak. She only waited, and Pierre Vallon added with a faint smile:

"The permit includes you and me, Maria and Jacques, and a member of my Orchestra who was unfortunately damaged by the collapse of a burning house!"

Zoia gave a little cry of sheer relief.

"Oh, Papa! How did you manage it, and how dared you go to the Emperor?"

"I asked to see him, and he remembered me," Pierre Vallon replied. "We talked of the last time I played in Paris, and then I explained to him the predicament I was in because you were with me."

Zoia made a little sound but she did not interrupt, and Pierre Vallon went on:

"The Emperor said: 'I can understand your anxiety, and I suppose I must let you go, although I would have liked you to stay and play for me.'

" 'I hope to do that in happier times, Your Majesty,' I answered.

" 'I look forward to it,' the Emperor said. 'The Opera House in Paris is waiting for you.' "

Zoia clasped her hands together.

"That was very complimentary, Papa, but how will we be able to get away?"

"Jacques has kept our two carriages hidden, which was fortunate because practically every vehicle in the city was commandeered by those who left before the French arrived."

"And horses?" Zoia asked.

"They too are in a safe place," her father answered. "I have decided that it would be safest for us to leave at dawn. The Emperor has promised us an escort of soldiers, and at such an early hour we are less likely to become involved with those who are robbing anyone they find on the streets."

As he spoke, he thought of the horrifying spectacles he had seen when he and Jacques had gone to the Kremlin to find the Emperor.

Everywhere they looked they had seen French soldiers staggering from houses, laden not only with money and jewels but with boots, linen, and women's furs and cloaks.

They had also seen people walking the streets robbed of their clothes, and those resisting being savagely beaten.

They had learnt that the French were pillaging the Churches, and any woman who was not old and decrepit was seized and carrried away, regardless of her shrieks and struggles.

Although Pierre Vallon did not say so, the flames of the burning city were now perilously close to the quiet little Square where he had bought his wife her "Doll's-House."

Zoia went upstairs and when she entered the Duke's bedroom she saw that he was awake and was watching her as she moved towards him.

"You have news?" he asked.

She did not ask him how he knew, for she was aware that they were so closely attuned that he knew what she was thinking, just as he had when she had played the piano.

"We leave at dawn tomorrow morning."

"*We?*"

"Papa has a special permit from the Emperor
Bonaparte himself for us to leave the city, and we are
to be escorted by soldiers."

"He has seen the Emperor?"

The Duke did not seem surprised.

"Yes, and he remembered him."

There was a faint smile on the Duke's lips as he
replied:

"Who could forget Pierre Vallon?"

As he spoke, Zoia wondered if when he was well
he would forget her, but she dared not ask the question.

"Where are we going?" the Duke enquired now.

Zoia looked startled.

"I forgot to ask Papa. It did not seem important, as
long as we leave Moscow."

"Tell your father to make for Odessa. I know the
Governor and it should be easy from there to find a
ship to carry us home."

The Duke closed his eyes again, as if talking was
still an effort, and Zoia stood indecisively beside the
bed.

"To carry us home!"

Did he mean by that to *his* home? To England?

She longed to ask him to explain, then was afraid
of the answer.

Of course, what he really meant was that because
England had command of the Seas, there would be
English ships there which would be only too honoured
to carry back to their own country anyone as important as the Duke.

But to the English she and her father were enemies.

Because she felt that there was nothing she could
say, Zoia went to her own room, which was just

across the passage, and started to add to the things she had already packed.

Suddenly she felt that the only way she could express the conflict which raged within her was in music.

Because she felt that when the Duke was unconscious music might reach him when the human voice could not do so, she had persuaded Jacques to bring up to her bedroom the piano which was usually housed in the Salon.

There were two pianos in the house: the one her father preferred was in his special sanctum, and the other one, which she and her mother played, was also used to entertain their friends, who would seldom leave the house without begging Pierre Vallon to let them hear one of his compositions.

It stood now in an alcove in her bedroom, and, knowing that the doors of both rooms were open so that the Duke could listen, Zoia sat down on the stool.

She started to play very softly the music she had been playing that first day in the Ysevolsov Palace when he had come in to listen to her and had known what she was seeing as she played.

The melody, composed by her father, swept away her fear of the future and made her forget for a moment the fires raging outside and the smoke billowing up to the sky.

She was transported into a magical world of beauty and happiness, and only as she finished playing did she wonder if the Duke was asleep or whether he had listened and understood as he had done before.

As she wondered, she heard him call her name.

She ran from the piano across the passage and into his room.

As she went to his bedside, he put out his hand and she laid hers in it.

"You were playing that for me?" he asked in a deep voice.

"Yes."

"I thought so, and I remember how shocked I was the first time that it should have aroused such unusual feelings in me."

"And . . . now?"

"I think it was fate that brought us together; fate that we should not only meet but be here when history is being made, something we shall both of us remember for the rest of our lives."

While his fingers were holding hers it was difficult for Zoia to think of anything but the magic that she felt within herself because they were touching each other.

She was sure that the Duke was too ill to feel a magnetic rapture that was indescribable, as had happened before when their hands had touched.

But she realised that his eyes were on her face and she thought they were searching for something, but she was not certain what it was.

"Once we are free of Moscow, we will move very slowly," she said, "so that you will not be bumped unnecessarily or suffer too much discomfort."

"I know that you and Maria will look after me," the Duke said, "and I am greatly relieved that, owing to your father's cleverness, you are able to escape from Moscow."

Zoia looked down at him a little uncertainly.

Because his words were so formal she thought that she could not understand what he was thinking.

She had an impulse to go down on her knees beside the bed and tell him how much she loved him and that she would willingly sacrifice her life if it would make him better or keep him safe.

Then she thought that perhaps he would be embarrassed and would suggest that she behave in a more restrained manner.

She released his hand, walked to the window, and stood looking out blindly.

Then she saw that behind the houses on the other side of the Square there was the brilliant light of a raging fire, and she could even see flames rising every now and then above the grey buildings.

She heard her father coming up the stairs and a moment later he walked into the room.

"Zoia will have told Your Grace the news," he said to the Duke.

"As I said to you before," the Duke replied, "you will travel more safely and perhaps a great deal faster without me."

"On the contrary," Pierre Vallon replied, "I intend to go to Odessa, and we will then need your assistance to find some way of reaching France."

Zoia started.

So that was where he wished to go—to their home in France.

"I am sure something can be arranged," the Duke answered.

Zoia knew by the way he spoke that he was desperately tired.

"I think it would be wise," she said, "if I asked Jacques to cook you something light and you went to sleep as soon as possible. We all have to rise very early tomorrow morning."

The Duke did not reply, and without troubling him further Zoia went downstairs in search of Jacques.

* * *

When they were clear of Moscow and the four horses pulling their carriage were moving at a good rate, Zoia gave a sigh of relief that seemed to come from the very depths of her being.

Outside the windows was the unspoilt countryside and there were few people on the road.

She told her father of the Duke's idea that they should make for Odessa and found that it was what Pierre Vallon had decided to do.

"It would be impossible to travel into Europe accompanied by an Englishman," he said, "and I also think we are wise to travel to the South, where the weather will be warmer than it is likely to be here in a short time."

"That is true," Zoia agreed. "It often gets very cold in October."

"Last year it snowed at the end of September," her father replied, "and that is something the Emperor would be wise to remember."

Zoia had been surprised to find when morning came that her father, or perhaps Jacques, had engaged no less than eight servants to accompany them.

She did not ask where these Russians had been hiding but thought that perhaps it was the same place where Jacques had concealed their carriages and horses, which were strong and well bred.

Because she was so close to her father, she knew that he was very apprehensive that the soldiers who were to be their escort might take it upon themselves to commandeer the horses, which, after the slaughter at Borodino, were obviously in short supply.

But the French soldiers were not inclined or important enough to do anything but obey the orders they had been given, and soon after dawn they started to move towards the Rogozhskol Gate, which would take them out of the West Side of the city.

Fortunately, this did not require them to pass

through the centre, where most of the troops were quartered.

Nevertheless it was a nerve-racking drive, as, apart from the fear that some officious Frenchman might challenge them or a mob of drunken soldiers decide to pilfer the carriages, there was also the danger of the burning houses and the falling walls.

As they drove along, it looked to Zoia as if at least three-quarters of the houses they passed were in flames, but Jacques had said there were still parts of Moscow which had not been damaged.

Nevertheless, at times she could feel the burning heat of the flames almost scorching her face and when they reached the bridge over the river her father looked back with an expression that made her ask quickly:

"What has upset you, Papa?"

"The Grand Theatre was burning last night."

"Oh, Papa, I am sorry!"

"It is not surprising," he said. "It was built of wood and a year's supply of timber had been stacked against the walls."

He spoke almost without expression in his voice, but she knew how much it hurt him.

Again he was thinking of her mother and how pleased she had been when they first came to Moscow because the Theatre had seemed to be an ideal place for him to build up a great Orchestra in exactly the way he wanted it.

Deliberately, because she wanted to cheer him, Zoia made her voice sound light and almost happy as she said:

"We are starting a new chapter of our lives, Papa, and I have a feeling that it will be an interesting and exciting one for you."

Her father did not reply, and she could not help

remembering that she could not say the same thing for herself. But she knew that for the moment what mattered more than anything else was that the Duke was safe and that he still needed her.

Jacques had constructed a very comfortable bed in the larger of Pierre Vallon's carriages, using a board of wood stretching from the back seat to the smaller one opposite.

He had heaped on it two comfortable mattresses, and with the help of their new servants they had carried the Duke downstairs.

Careful though they had been, Zoia knew that the Duke found it extremely painful.

She had seen his lips tighten and the colour leave his face, but he said nothing except to thank those who had carried him to the carriage.

There was room for her to sit beside him and for her father to sit on the small seat opposite, but she was determined that once they were out of the city she would persuade her father to ride in the other carriage.

At the moment this contained only Maria and a number of small packages and parcels which she had insisted on taking with them at the last moment.

Their trunks had been strapped on the tops of the two carriages, and Zoia could not help thinking that it was fortunate that the Russians could not see the very elegant clothing which the Duke owned.

After his valet had been killed by the explosion, Prince Ysevolsov's servants had been sensible enough to take from the Tsar's carriage all the Duke's possessions.

The head servant who had escorted her to Moscow had been in the Prince's employment for many years and he understood the needs of a gentleman.

It would have been difficult otherwise, Zoia

thought, to provide the Duke, who was so tall and broad-shouldered, with the clothes he would need once he was on his feet again.

She and Maria had packed only the essentials for themselves for the journey.

There were many little things that Zoia would have liked to take with her because they reminded her of her mother or simply because she was fond of them, but she knew that to overload the horses on such a long journey might prevent them from reaching their destination safely.

She therefore restricted herself to packing only what she thought she would actually need and just a few of her prettiest gowns that were light and took up very little room.

What was more important than anything else was that they should have enough food, for Jacques thought that it might be difficult to buy much on the journey.

"When there's a war, people are frightened that they themselves will go hungry," he said to Zoia. "I can't have the Master getting ill, or you, *M'mselle,* for that matter."

He did not include the Duke in his solicitude and Zoia knew without being told that Jacques almost resented the strange man who he felt had intruded on the family atmosphere that had been so evident in their small household before the Duke had joined it.

"You must not forget our invalid, Jacques," she said aloud.

"We'll not do that, *M'mselle,*" Jacques replied.

But his voice was cold and had none of the warmth in it that she would have liked to hear.

Maria, however, thought that the Duke was the finest man she had ever seen, and when in his quiet voice he thanked her for dressing his wounds, she knew that he was suffering acutely and was overwhelmed by his bravery.

She would, Zoia knew, have done anything in her power to help him. But it was Jacques who was really responsible for the whole organisation of their journey from the moment they left Moscow.

When they were finally out of sight of the city and its spires and domes were no longer visible and there was only a great crimson glow in the sky from the fires, Pierre Vallon had an expression on his face which told Zoia that a composition was forming in his mind.

She knew the signs so well, and as soon as it was possible to do so, she stopped the carriage and persuaded her father to change places with Maria.

If he was composing he would want to be alone, and she felt too that not only would he be more comfortable, but she would be able to talk with the Duke without feeling that every word they said was overheard.

From the moment Pierre Vallon had realised that it would be impossible for the Duke to leave them without the certainty of being arrested and maybe killed for being English, he had not referred to Zoia's feelings for him again.

She knew, however, that he was still afraid that she would break her heart over a man who could never really be of any consequence in her life.

But, as if he realised that further discussion would only disrupt the closeness of their own relationship and have little effect, Pierre Vallon had, in his characteristic manner, tried to divorce his mind from the problem.

It would be a great relief, Zoia told herself, if he could really concentrate on his music, because that meant that she would no longer feel guilty or that she was in any way defying her father, whom she loved so devotedly.

The carriages started off again, and Maria, after fussing a little over the Duke, sat back and almost immediately fell asleep.

Travelling by carriage always made her sleepy, and Zoia thought with a little smile that now she was, to all intents and purposes, alone with the man she loved.

She expected him to sleep, but when she looked at the Duke she found that he· was watching her with his grey eyes.

"You are comfortable?" she asked.

"I am thinking how fortunate I am not to have been left to die at Borodino."

"Forget about it," Zoia said. "I have told Papa that we are starting a new chapter in our lives, and I do not want to think any more of the terrible casualties to both Armies, or that Moscow is burning."

The Duke did not answer, and after a moment she said:

"There will be problems in the future, of course, but they will be new problems, and perhaps we shall feel like the snakes that shed their old skins and emerge with new ones."

"I like your skin just as it is," the Duke said quietly.

She blushed because she was not expecting a compliment from him.

After a moment he went on:

"You are a very remarkable person, Zoia. I know of no other woman who would take what has happened these past few weeks so calmly or leave their home to burn to the ground without complaining about it with tears."

"I mind . . . of course I mind!" Zoia replied. "But I

have saved the only things that are important to me
... Papa ... and you!"

She said the last two words very softly and did not
look at the Duke as she spoke, but she was aware
that his eyes were on her face and she wondered what
he was thinking.

After a silence of some minutes, she turned to look
at him and saw that once again he was asleep.

* * *

Afterwards it was hard for Zoia to remember the
details of the long journey from Moscow to Odessa.

They could not travel very far every day because
the horses had to rest and there was no possibility of
changing them as there had been on the journey from
St. Petersburg to Moscow.

In fact, owing to the war, horses were in such short
supply that one of the servants had to be on watch
every night for fear that the horses might be stolen,
or, worse still, that they themselves might be attacked
by robbers.

When they got farther south it grew warmer and
there were vineyards where the grapes were being cut
in the hot sunshine. There was fruit on the trees and
flowers everywhere and Zoia found it enchanting.

Soon there were no further obvious signs of war, of
soldiers being marched to the north to join Kutuzov's
Army, or only women working in the fields as their
men had been taken from them for Military Service.

Instead, there were peasants who greeted them
with smiles and were willing to sell them any fresh food
they wished to buy.

The horses were getting tired but Zoia felt a new
vitality and energy seeping through her.

She knew that it sprang from her happiness be-

cause the Duke was there and every day he seemed to
grow stronger.

They would talk together or sit in silence, and yet
they knew that they were communicating without
words and there was a closeness between them which
she dared not try to analyse.

Jacques had brought tents in which they could sleep
at night, or, if it seemed easier and more comfortable,
she and Maria shared one carriage while her father
slept beside the Duke.

It was then that Zoia would lie awake in the darkness and know that her love for the Duke had increased every hour, every minute, that she had been
beside him.

It was not because of what he said, nor was it for
any reason which she could explain to herself.

It was just because her whole being went out towards him as the man she had always wanted to find,
the man she had loved secretly in her music long before she met him.

'I am happy,' she thought, 'happier than I have
ever been in my whole life, and as far as I am concerned this journey can go on forever, into eternity,
and I shall be content!'

But finally, because everything must come to an
end, they saw Odessa ahead of them, and her father
said when they were lunching beside the road:

"We will take Your Grace to the Governor-
General's Palace, then you and I will find somewhere
to stay."

Zoia started at her father's words and, without real-
ising that she was doing so, looked pleadingly at the
Duke.

"What are you saying?" the Duke enquired. "Of
course you must come with me. As you must be aware,
I cannot possibly do without you."

"I think it would be better, Your Grace, if we stayed on our own," Pierre Vallon replied. "After all, for all you know, the Governor-General may look upon me as an enemy of his people, which indeed my countrymen are!"

The Duke smiled.

"The Governor-General is in fact a Frenchman."

Pierre Vallon looked astonished, and the Duke explained:

"The *Duc* de Richelieu was an emigré during the Revolution and entered Russian service. In 1803 he became Governor-General of New Russia, as they call the Ukraine, and he was responsible for the development of the port of Odessa, which I know will impress you."

As Pierre Vallon still looked surprised, the Duke finished by saying:

"I am assured that you will both find a warm welcome waiting for you at the Palace."

But Pierre Vallon still hesitated before he said:

"If you will promise me that we are not of the slightest embarrassment to Your Grace, then Zoia and I will be honoured to accompany you."

"May I also inform you," the Duke said, "that the Governor-General is extremely musical. In fact, last time I was in Odessa some years ago, I remember being excessively bored by the Concert I had to attend when I was staying in his Palace."

Pierre Vallon laughed.

"That, of course, is an undeniable recommendation! At the same time, Your Grace, I understood that you were fond of music."

"Very fond, when it is the right sort!" the Duke replied. "And let me add that I am looking forward to hearing what you have been composing while we have been travelling here."

"I shall be delighted to play it to you," Pierre Vallon replied, "but actually it requires a large Orchestra."

"I expect the Governor-General will be able to supply that!" the Duke answered.

"Are you so sure that your friends will welcome us?" Zoia asked. "They may think us an intolerable nuisance, or perhaps the Palace is full."

"Wait until you see it," the Duke replied.

They arrived the following afternoon and as Zoia saw the tall cypress-tress, which had first been introduced by Catherine the Great, silhouetted against a translucent sky with the sea beyond, she thought she had never seen anything so lovely as the Governor-General's Palace.

She was spellbound by its gleaming white beauty, surrounded by flowers and shrubs that were a kaleidoscope of colour.

As they drove up to the Palace, Zoia could not help thinking that in contrast she looked dusty and travel-stained, while she knew that the Duke himself was very tired.

Nevertheless, when the servants fetched first one of the Governor-General's Aides-de-Camp, then His Excellency himself, there was no doubt of their welcome, and Pierre Vallon need not have been afraid that he and Zoia were an embarrassment.

"I heard you conduct in London," the Governor-General said, "and I can assure you, *Monsieur* Vallon, that nothing could give me greater pleasure than to offer you my hospitality."

When the Duke presented Zoia, the Frenchman appraised her with shrewd eyes and said:

"There is one very easy way, *Mademoiselle,* into the heart of Odessa, and that is beauty!"

Zoia blushed, but there was no doubt of his admiration or the manner in which he continued to look at her as they entered the Palace.

The Duke was too tired to do anything but fall asleep as soon as he was shown to his bedroom and helped into bed. But Zoia, after having enjoyed a warm bath, put on one of her prettiest gowns and went downstairs.

The Governor-General's wife, the *Duchesse* de Richelieu, made them welcome, although some of the other women staying in the Palace were not so effusive, sensing her as a rival and knowing that they could not compete with her in looks.

But the fact that they had come from Moscow and had news of the battle which had only just been reported in Odessa made Pierre Vallon the focus of attention, and he had to explain in detail all that had occured, besides recounting his own interview with the Emperor Napoleon.

"How can he behave in such an uncivilised way?" the *Duchesse* asked. "He is nothing but a Corsican barbarian and a savage."

"I agree with you, my dear," the Governor-General said. "At the same time, one has to admit that it was an amazing feat of generalship to lead six hundred thousand men such a distance and to enter Moscow without resistance from anyone."

"I only hope he is burnt to death with all those lovely houses!" one of the guests exclaimed. "I had intended to go to Moscow this winter for the Balls."

"There will certainly be no Balls," Pierre Vallon answered, "and I doubt if by the time the French leave there will be anything left standing, except perhaps the Kremlin!"

"Why should the French leave?" the *Duchesse* enquired.

"They will have to go," Pierre Vallon answered,

"for there is not enough food to last for long except perhaps for members of the Staff; what is left of the Russian population, hiding in the Churches and in cellars, is already on the verge of starvation."

"It does not bear thinking about," one of the women guests cried. "I only hope that all the French —every single one of that detestable nation—will sooner or later die like rats in a trap!"

There was an uncomfortable silence after she had spoken, as the lady remembered that both the Governor-General and Pierre Vallon were French.

Then everybody started to talk hurriedly at once.

* * *

In the next few days Zoia suffered no embarrassment and received nothing but kindness even from the Russian guests in the Palace.

"You have Russian eyes, my dear," one old Countess said to her, "and I know that like your grandmother and your mother, you feel things very deeply."

She gave a little sigh.

"That is to us Russians our glory and our curse. We so often touch ecstasy, but we also know despair. You cannot have one without the other."

"I suppose not, Ma'am," Zoia replied.

She knew it was ecstasy to be with the Duke, to see him, to talk to him, but it was the darkness of despair to know that as he got better day by day, the time when they could be together was running out.

As soon as he had recovered from the strenuous journey, he was well enough to dress and just to sit on the balcony of his large bedroom, which overlooked the garden and the sea.

A few days later he was carried downstairs to sit on the verandah.

"It is so beautiful here!" Zoia said.

As she spoke she listened to the birds and felt a touch of salt on the warm air, which came from the waves moving restlessly over the sea, vividly blue against the sunlit sky.

"There is only one thing missing," the Duke replied.

"What is that?" she asked.

"Your music."

"Do you want me to play to you?"

"I would like you to do so."

She had seen a piano in the room behind them, and without saying any more she walked towards it and sat down.

The windows were all open and she could see the Duke as she played and she thought he should listen to one of her father's compositions which described so vividly the beauty of nature.

Then when she started playing, without really being conscious of it she expressed in the music which her father had composed not what he had felt but what she herself was feeling.

Despite every resolution not to do so, her love crept into her fingers and with it the ecstasy and despair that the Countess had described so accurately.

There was the ecstasy she had felt from the moment she had met the Duke and when his hand had first touched hers, a sensation so perfect, so beautiful, that it was part of the Divine, and yet it was also a very human part of herself because she was a woman and he was a man.

She told him in her playing how she had always believed that one day she would find love as her mother had done; one day the man who had been only a dream in her heart would materialise.

Now it was real—very real—and when she had first seen him she recognised him because already she had loved him for years, or perhaps it was for centuries, in other lives.

Then as her love flowed from her fingers there was the despair too, the knowledge that inevitably, inescapably, they must part.

She told him how if she never saw him again her heart would always be with him, her prayers would protect him, and what he had evoked in her would go on living eternally because it was an indivisible part of her life.

As always when she was playing and was carried away by the music, Zoia forgot everything except what she must express because it swept from her like the waters of the sea.

When she finished, it seemed as if there was nothing more to say, and she was suddenly exhausted because she had poured her very self into the music she had created.

Only then did she realise that there were a number of people listening to her, including her father.

They had moved into the verandah and were sitting beside the Duke. They had made no noise, but listened in silence because it was impossible for anyone not to be moved by what they heard.

Then as Zoia came back from the world into which she had been carried by her own creation, she saw her father's face and knew that she had revealed what she felt so clearly that he was deeply touched by what he had learnt and at the same time apprehensive.

With a feeling of consternation and also one of shyness which seeped deep into her soul, Zoia realised that she had betrayed herself.

Rising to her feet, without explanation or apology she left the room, moving as if in a dream along the passages of the Palace and up the stairs to the sanctuary of her own bedroom.

Chapter Seven

Going to her bedroom to dress for dinner, Zoia saw lying on the bed the beautiful train that the *Duchesse* had given her.

It was three days ago that the Governor-General had said at luncheon:

"Our most distinguished guest, the Duke of Welminster, tells me that he feels well enough to enjoy a party. I therefore intend to invite all the people to meet him who have been longing to do so since they learnt that he had arrived in Odessa."

"A party? What sort of party?" the *Duchesse* enquired from the other end of the table.

The Governor-General smiled.

"Just the sort you enjoy, my dear, with dancing and of course, for *Monsieur* Vallon's benefit, the best musicians obtainable in New Russia."

"Dancing!" the ladies exclaimed in unison, and went on to add:

"What you are saying, Your Excellency, is that you are going to give a Ball."

"A Ball it shall be," the Governor-General promised,

"and I hope our Imperial Splendour is as magnificent as His Grace enjoyed in St. Petersburg."

The Duke smiled.

"Everybody was very sober-minded in St. Petersburg," he said. "In fact, when I was staying with His Imperial Majesty there were no Balls, only Receptions at which everybody gossiped eternally on the same subject."

"I shall issue a decree," the Governor-General said, "that no-one is to speak of war and we are all to be entirely frivolous and light-hearted!"

Listening, Zoia thought it would be very exciting to be present at a Ball such as her mother had often described to her.

She was well aware that it would be very splendid and everything would glitter from the crystal chandeliers to the bejewelled guests.

But she knew with an ache in her heart that now that the Duke was well, he would be planning to leave Odessa, and the moment when she would see him for the last time was approaching nearer and nearer.

The only person who did not seem to be very enthusiastic about the idea of a Ball was her father, but he had always disliked formal parties and Zoia suspected that he would not be very impressed by any musicians that the Governor-General would engage to entertain him.

At the same time, woman-like, she immediately began to consider what she should wear.

She wanted the Duke to admire her and it would be very humiliating to feel that she was outshone in every way by the other ladies staying in the Palace.

Fortunately, amongst the things which she had brought with her from Moscow was one very elaborate evening-gown which in fact she had never worn.

She had been keeping it for the Winter Balls which

the Governor, Count Rostopchin, gave in the Kremlin.

She had been invited last year, and though she was in mourning for her mother, she had thought it would be very exciting to accompany her father to such a function.

So she and Maria had planned together a very beautiful and elaborate white gown that she hoped would gain her father's approval.

She knew, from what her mother had told her, that if the Governor-General's Ball in Odessa was to rival those given in St. Petersburg, the ladies would all have trains.

This was something she did not possess and she wondered if she should explain her lack to her hostess, then decided against it.

She had, however, been sent for yesterday evening by the *Duchesse*. When she reached the Governor-General's State Apartments, she found her hostess lying on a couch in the window, wearing an attractive negligé.

"Sit down, child," she said. "I want to talk to you. There does not seem to have been a moment since you arrived for us to have a chat."

"It is very kind of you, *Madame*, to have my father and myself to stay," Zoia replied.

"Your father is my husband's concern," the *Duchesse* replied, "but you, because you are your mother's daughter, are mine."

"You knew my mother?" Zoia asked, her eyes lighting up.

"I met her in France just after she had married your father and before my husband and I had to flee the country unless we wished to be guillotined."

She put out her hand to take Zoia's and said gently:

"Now she is no longer with you, and I know you must miss her. You are very like her."

Zoia's eyes filled with tears at the sympathetic note in the *Duchesse's* voice, and because she found it impossible to speak, the *Duchesse* went on:

"I know that in the circumstances in which you find yourself at the moment, your mother would wish you to enjoy the Ball that is taking place tomorrow night. You must therefore allow me to give you a train to wear, which, as I expect you know, is correct on such occasions."

"I knew that, *Madame,* and I was feeling embarrassed because I did not have one," Zoia replied.

"That is why I must fill your need," the *Duchesse* said. "Look in the next room on the bed and see if you like what you see."

Zoia went from the *Duchesse's* Boudoir into her bedroom and saw laying on the huge carved and canopied bed the loveliest train she could ever have imagined.

It was of turquoise-blue silk embroidered with pearls and narrowly edged with snow-white ermine.

She stared at it in delight, then went back to her hostess to say:

"It is beautiful! Really beautiful! Are you quite certain, *Madame*, that you wish to give me anything so valuable? Perhaps I should just borrow it for the evening."

"It is a gift," the *Duchesse* said, "and I have a brooch which matches it which I would like you to wear."

She opened a velvet-lined box which she had beside her and Zoia saw a brooch fashioned of turquoise and diamonds in a very delicate design which made her exclaim in delight.

She pinned it in the front of the gown she was wearing at the moment and said:

"I cannot begin to thank you for such lovely presents, and I am sure the turquoises will bring me luck, as I believe they are reputed to do."

"Here and in the Caucasus they are considered to be very lucky," the *Duchesse* agreed, "and perhaps that is what you are looking for at the moment."

Zoia did not answer, but the *Duchesse* saw the sadness in her eyes, and she said quietly:

"Life has been difficult for you, especially when the two nations to which you belong are at war with each other, but I have a feeling that you will find happiness when you least expect it."

"I hope . . . so," Zoia said in a low voice.

Then, because she had no wish to discuss the Duke with anyone, she thanked the *Duchesse* again for her presents and went to her own room.

When she was alone, she asked herself how was it possible for her ever to find happiness when she must lose the Duke.

Every day that he had grown stronger she had been glad, both for his sake and because she felt that she had been partly instrumental in his regaining his health so quickly.

At the same time, she knew that it carried her inevitably nearer to the time when they must part.

She wondered how she could bear actually to say the word "good-bye," and she was afraid that when the moment came, she would break down and collapse sobbing at his feet.

Then she told herself that her pride would prevent her from doing anything but behaving in a dignified and proper manner.

It was pride that came from the blood of the Strovolskys and their ancient heritage, and it was also very much part of her father because he had achieved so much with his great talent.

At the same time, when she walked with the Duke

in the garden and listened to him talking to her in his deep voice, she knew that her love was so over-whelming, so intense, that it was hard to behave as he would expect her to do.

How, she asked herself at times, had anyone ever called her an Ice Maiden when her whole body seemed to burn with hidden fires and she had an uncontrollable urge to express her love because it filled her mind, her heart, and her soul to the exclusion of all else.

Ever since the day she had played to the Duke and revealed if not to him then to her father the depth and breadth of her feelings, she had not touched the piano.

She did not trust herself and she still felt shy and ashamed at the manner in which she had been carried away into proclaiming what she felt.

"It was indiscreet and foolish!" she berated herself.

But she felt sometimes that if she did not express the fires that consumed her, she would explode like the gun which had exploded and injured the Duke.

Then in the quiet of the night, she would tell her-self that the practical, sensible French side of her nature must control the impetuous wildness of the Russian side.

Yet in fact there was not one part of her that was not desperately, overwhelmingly in love.

* * *

The maid had prepared a bath for Zoia and it was scented with perfume which smelled to her like tube-roses, the flowers of passion.

As she lay in the warm water, it was impossible not to think of the Duke and repeat in her mind the things he had talked about as they had wandered round the garden earlier in the day.

There were other people in the house-party doing

the same thing, and although they moved out of ear-
shot Zoia was very conscious that they were never
completely alone.

"You are really better?" she asked. "The Ball tonight will not be too much for you?"

"Maria asked me the same question," the Duke
answered, "but even she has had to admit that my
wounds are healed and she can no longer molly-coddle
me any more than you can."

"I have no . . . wish to do . . . that."

As she spoke, Zoia knew that it was not the truth.
She wanted to keep him helpless, simply so that she
and Maria should be indispensable to him.

"My wounds are healed," the Duke went on, "but
I shall carry the scars as decorations, or should I say
souvenirs, of the battle of Borodino for the rest of my
life."

"It is something I have no wish to remember,"
Zoia replied. "When the servants brought you to our
house in Moscow, I . . . thought you were . . . dead."

"I was not meant to die," the Duke said lightly,
"and one day I shall tell you why."

She glanced at him questioningly, wondering what
he would tell her, but he was not looking at her but
across the garden at the sea, stretching away towards
the horizon.

'He is thinking of his home in England,' she thought
with a little contraction of her heart.

She wondered if she should ask him how soon he
intended to leave Odessa.

Then she knew that she could not bear to hear the
answer. It was too painful and she might even betray
her true feelings when she learnt the actual date of
his departure.

"I think I shall always remember the beauty of

this garden," the Duke said aloud, "and that you look like one of the flowers in it."

Their eyes met, and for a moment it seemed as if they were as close as they had been when he had listened to her music and known what she was thinking.

Then before she could speak, before they could say anything more to each other, they were joined by people who wanted to talk about the Ball.

After her bath, Zoia sat in front of the mirror while her maid arranged her hair in the more fashionable style she had worn in Moscow.

Amongst her mother's jewellery that she had brought away with her was a lovely wreath of diamonds which Natasha Strovolsky had been given on her seventeenth birthday.

Reverently Zoia had taken it from its wrappings, and she felt that if she wore it tonight, her mother would be thinking of her, at the first big Ball she had ever attended.

Zoia had seen her mother wearing the wreath on various occasions when she had accompanied her father to some distinguished function to which she was too young to be invited.

"You look like the Fairy Princess, Mama!" she had said once. "And Papa is, of course, Prince Charming."

"That is what he has always been to me," her mother replied.

She put up her hand and touched the wreath on her head and said with a smile:

"I am so glad that I can hold my own with all the important and distinguished people who will be there tonight. I so very nearly sold this when we first married and were very poor before your father was recognised as a great musician, but he insisted on my keeping it and now I am glad that I did."

It was not because it was valuable, Zoia knew, but because it stood for everything that her mother had given up for love.

'That was Mama's Imperial Splendour,' she thought. 'Tonight it will be mine and perhaps I shall never go to a Ball like this again.'

She was certain that when they reached France, with the war still raging there would be few festive occasions at which people would be dressed as they would be tonight.

With the wreath on her head, she certainly looked very regal, and the maid helped her first into her gown, then fixed the exquisite turquoise-blue train to her shoulders.

It gave her a presence and a dignity she had never had before, but as she looked at her reflection in the mirror, all she wondered was what the Duke would think of her.

The door opened and her father came into the room.

"You are ready, Papa?" Zoia asked.

She turned from the mirror so that he could look at her.

"I want to speak to you," Pierre Vallon said.

Her expression changed. She made a gesture to the maid to leave the room, then waited until the door had shut behind her.

"What is it, Papa?"

He walked towards her and she knew instinctively that he was feeling for words.

"What . . . is it?" she asked again.

"There is a Turkish ship in the port," Pierre Vallon replied. "It will leave on the dawn tide."

Zoia drew in her breath.

"I have spoken to the Captain," her father went on, "and he will take us to Marseilles. It is an opportunity we cannot afford to miss."

"But, Papa . . . !" Zoia began.

He interrupted her.

"Before you say anything, let me tell you that a British Man-o'-War is expected in two or three days' time. I heard the Duke telling one of His Excellency's Aides-de-Camp that he intended to ask for passage on it to England."

Zoia was very still. Then she sat down on the stool she had just vacated, feeling that her legs would no longer carry her.

"What I want you to do," Pierre Vallon said, "is to leave the Ball and drive straight to the ship, where I will be waiting for you."

"Leave the . . . Ball?" Zoia repeated stupidly.

"It would be wisest, my dear," he said. "What is the point of torturing yourself by saying good-bye to the Duke, knowing that there will be nothing to gain from it but added unhappiness to what you are feeling already."

"You know . . . how much I . . . love him, Papa."

"Yes, I know," Pierre Vallon said, "but as you agreed from the very beginning, there can be no happy ending to your story. Therefore, I think my method of leaving is kinder for you and for him."

"Kinder for . . . him?" Zoia questioned.

"What can he do but thank you?" Pierre Vallon asked. "The Duke of Welminster is as important in England as your grandfather was in Russia. They both had a pride in their family and their blood which would not allow them to lower their standards of behaviour for anything—not even for love!"

Zoia clenched her fingers together until the knuckles showed white.

She knew that what her father was saying to her was true, but that made it no less hurtful, no less an instrument of despair.

"You have to be brave, dearest," Pierre Vallon said, "and quite frankly, this will be the easiest way."

He did not wait for her answer but went on:

"I have spoken to Maria. She is already packing. She and Jacques will leave the Palace late in the evening and drive to the ship."

Zoia waited, knowing that what he was to tell her to do was, as it were, the fall of the axe.

"I will be waiting at the end of the garden for you, in a closed carriage," Pierre Vallon said. "It might evoke awkward questions if we leave the Ball-Room together."

'Perhaps the Duke would stop us,' Zoia thought.

But she knew there was no point in saying such a thing aloud and she merely went on listening as her father continued:

"I understand that the Governor-General has arranged for a Gypsy Orchestra to play at about midnight and for their women to dance. I am sorry we shall miss it, but I suggest that as soon as everybody's attention is concentrated on them, you slip away through the garden to where I shall be waiting for you."

"It ... seems very ... rude," Zoia murmured, because she thought something was expected of her.

"I have already thought of that," Pierre Vallon replied. "I have written a letter both to the Governor-General and to the *Duchesse,* thanking them for their hospitality."

"And the ... Duke?"

Zoia could not help the question, which seemed to burst from her lips.

"When the Duke learns that we have gone," Pierre Vallon replied, "he will appreciate our tact and the way we have saved him from being involved in something which might prove uncomfortably emotional."

There was a cynical twist to his lips as he added:

"The English dislike anything which might break down their traditional reserve."

"You really do not think he will . . . consider it . . . unkind and . . . remiss of us not to tell him what we are . . . doing?" Zoia asked

"Do you want me to be frank with you?" Pierre Vallon enquired.

"Of course, Papa!"

"Then if I am honest," he said, "I know that the Duke finds you very beautiful and very desirable, but we have to face the truth, my dearest, and know that he wants more than that in the woman he will make his wife."

Zoia shut her eyes, as if to protect herself from a blow. Then she said in a voice that even to herself sounded dull with misery:

"I will do what you . . . want me to do . . . Papa . . . because I trust you . . . and perhaps it is right that we should save the Duke . . . any embarrassment."

"You are very sensible, my dearest," Pierre Vallon said, "and believe me, if I could save you from what you are suffering, if I could add your despair to my own and leave you free, I would do so."

His words brought Zoia to her feet.

She moved into his arms and put her cheek against his.

"I thought . . . love meant happiness . . . and joy," she said, "but what I am . . . feeling is a . . . darkness in which I am sure the sun will . . . never shine again."

"That is how I felt when your mother died," Pierre Vallon said, "but life goes on, and perhaps one day you will find somebody else you can love and be happy with."

Zoia wanted to cry out that that would never happen, but because she did not wish to upset her father, she said nothing, and she found a little comfort from his arms.

They stood entwined for a long moment, until Pierre Vallon said in a practical tone:

"We must not be late for dinner. His Excellency is making this a very special evening for us, as well as for the Duke, which of course I appreciate."

He went from the room and Zoia returned to the dressing-table to stand looking at her reflection in the mirror.

She was only surprised that her appearance seemed not to have changed.

She had a feeling that her father had taken away her youth, and she would not have been astonished to see herself old, wrinkled, and grey-haired.

Instead, she looked very lovely, except that deep in the purple depths of her eyes there was an inexpressible pain.

* * *

The Ball-Room with its huge chandeliers, each holding hundreds of tapers, was fragrant with flowers, and on the carved and gilt cornice which encircled the room there were also lines of lighted candles, something which Zoia had never seen before.

If the setting was magnificent, so were the guests.

Never had she imagined that women could wear so many glittering jewels, from the magnificent tiaras on their heads to the buckles on their shoes.

The *Duchesse* and her Ladies-in-Waiting were wearing the Russian Court dress of white silk, low, with a close-fitting bodice and a red train with gold embroidery.

They also wore the Ribbon of the Order of St. Catherine with its diamond cross.

And the men were determined not to be outdone,

for everyone present was either in a spectacular and splendid uniform or was covered with decorations and with ribbons across their chests. The Duke wore the Garter below the knee of his left leg.

There were Huzzar Officers in white and gold, Court Chamberlains in blue frock-coats stiff with gold, and young Circassians in high black or white sheepskin hats.

The evening was a fairy-tale spectacle, Zoia knew, from the moment she entered the huge Dining-Room to see a breathtaking display of gold plate on the table and to find, to her astonishment, that she was seated on the right of the Governor-General.

The Duke was on the right of the *Duchesse,* with Pierre Vallon on her left, and the Governor-General explained that she and her father, like the Duke, were the Guests of Honour of the evening.

"Everybody here has come to meet you," he said with a smile.

"Despite the fact that we are French?" Zoia asked in a low voice.

"As I am," the Governor-General replied. "My dear, music is an international language which knows no boundaries and no barriers, and in my estimation your father is King of a far greater Empire than anything Napoleon Bonaparte is trying to achieve."

Her father was certainly enjoying himself, Zoia thought, and she felt that for her too it would have been the most wonderful evening she had ever known, except that it was the end of the chapter about which she had spoken to the Duke as they had left Moscow.

'A very short . . . chapter,' she thought wistfully.

She could not help feeling that those that came after would be pale and uninspiring, and she shrank from thinking of what it would mean when she would never see the Duke again.

'I shall be alone as I have never been alone before,' she thought, 'and loneliness without love will be colder than any Siberian winter!'

The Duke was looking so magnificent that she found it difficult to see anyone else in the glittering company, and when they entered the Ball-Room he came to her side to say:

"I cannot ask you to dance with me, Zoia, for I have been forbidden by Maria to do anything so adventurous. But will you sit and talk to me?"

"You know I would like to do that," she answered.

She thought she would go with him there and then, but the Governor-General asked her to dance and it was impossible to refuse what was in effect a Royal Command.

When that dance was over there were other inescapable partners, and it was over an hour before finally the Duke came to her side and without saying anything they moved away together through the wide open windows of the Ball-Room and onto the terrace outside.

It was a night of stars with a crescent moon moving up the sky, and the garden with soft lights concealed amongst the flowers was a poem of beauty. Beyond, there was the mystery of the sea.

As they sat down on a seat in the shadows they could hear the music in the Ball-Room behind them and for a moment Zoia could find nothing to say, until the Duke asked:

"You are worried?"

"H-how do you . . . know I am?"

"I thought we had agreed long ago that I can read your thoughts."

Zoia did not reply because she was hoping that at this particular moment he could do no such thing. She felt something like panic sweep over her, only to reassure herself that she was being needlessly afraid.

It was one thing for him to understand what she played on the piano, but quite another to be aware that within an hour or so they would never see each other again.

"Are you going to tell me what is troubling you, or must I guess?" the Duke asked.

"Why . . . why should I be troubled by . . . anything?" she replied. "It is a . . . wonderful evening and a great . . . tribute to you."

"And of course to you," he replied. "Do I have to tell you how lovely you look?"

There was a note in his voice which made her vibrate to him. Then she told herself that he was just being polite, and she forced herself to say:

"Everybody has been . . . so kind. . . . Her Excellency gave me this beautiful train . . . and I shall always remember this moment . . . here in Odessa."

"There are other moments for us to remember," the Duke said.

"Will you . . . remember . . . them?" Zoia enquired.

She could not help the question because she wanted so much to hear the answer.

"I think what I will remember most vividly," he said, "is when I came back to consciousness after I had been wounded and saw your face looking down at me."

Zoia felt herself quiver. She had longed for him to talk to her like this, and yet there had never seemed to be an opportunity until now.

"I have a feeling," the Duke went on, "that you were calling me back through the darkness which encompassed me. I knew, when I thought about it, that even in my unconsciousness I had been conscious of you."

That was what she had wanted him to feel, she

thought, when she had called him desperately back to life from the darkness of death.

"Do you really think that is something I could ever forget?" the Duke asked.

"Please . . . remember me . . . always!"

The words were spoken impulsively and there was a pleading expression in her face as she looked up at the Duke.

His eyes met hers and he looked deep into her heart and they were both very still.

Then as if it came from another world, a voice said:

"Here you are, *Mademoiselle* Vallon! I have been looking for you. His Excellency wishes you to dance the mazourka with him."

For a moment Zoia found it hard to understand what was being said. Then as if she jerked herself back to reality, she rose to her feet.

"It is . . . very kind of His Excellency," she managed to say to the Aide-de-camp who had been sent in search of her.

"Let me escort you to the Ball-Room, *Mademoiselle.*"

"Thank you," Zoia replied.

She could not look at the Duke. She felt only as if she was being dragged away from him. She wanted to hold on to him and beg him not to let her go.

Instead, she followed the Aide-de-Camp back into the Ball-Room, thanked the Governor-General for his kindness, and they started the mazourka together in an animated manner.

After that it seemed impossible to escape from the men who surrounded her.

Every time a dance ended she looked round her frantically for the Duke, but before she could see him or move towards him through the crowds, somebody else had already claimed her and she was forced to dance with them.

She danced automatically and had no idea what her partners said to her or what she said to them. She was conscious only that time was going faster and faster and that all she wanted was to spend the last minutes with the man she loved.

Then despairingly she realised that there was no sign of her father either, and she knew where he had gone.

The dance came to an end. Now there was a roll of drums and on the steps into the Ball-Room there appeared a Gypsy Orchestra resplendent in their colourful clothes.

Their black eyes echoed their black hair, and their high cheek-bones singled them out as people of another race and, as Zoia knew, another culture.

The guests were all moving away from the centre of the floor, the older women seating themselves on the chairs and sofas round the room, the gentlemen standing beside them or in groups, waiting to applaud the entertainment that their host had provided.

Then as the gypsy women with their full skirts, gold necklaces, and jingling bracelets danced onto the floor with bare feet, Zoia knew this was the moment when she had to go.

She looked round once more, hoping to see the Duke and yet knowing that if she did so, there was nothing she could do about it.

It was too late now for them to talk, and besides, what was there to say, except that she loved him?

It was easy, while everybody's attention was fixed on the gypsies, for her to slip through one of the open windows onto the terrace where there were white marble steps going down into the garden.

There was nobody to notice her moving down them,

and she crossed the smooth green lawn between the beds of flowers until she saw another flight of steps.

As she reached them, she looked down and saw, as she had expected, a carriage.

It was closed and there were two men on the box, one of whom jumped down as soon as she appeared and went to the carriage-door.

Feeling as if she walked to her doom, Zoia descended the steps.

The door of the carriage was open, and, moving into the darkness inside, she sat down on the back seat, aware as she did so that her father was there waiting for her.

The carriage-door was shut, the footman climbed up onto the box, and the horses started off.

Zoia bent forward to take one last look through the window at the garden she had just left.

"Good-bye . . . my love . . . my only love . . . now and for eternity!" she said in her heart.

Then as she leant back in the seat, fighting against the tears which blinded her eyes, a deep voice asked:

"To whom are you saying good-bye, Zoia?"

She gave a cry both of shock and astonishment, for it was not her father who spoke, but the Duke!

She turned her face towards him, and in the light of the lamps on the drive down which they were travelling she could see his face and his eyes looking into hers.

For a moment she was incapable of speech, then almost incoherently she asked:

"Why . . . are you . . . here? What . . . has happened?"

"That is really the question I should ask you," the Duke replied. "How could you imagine that you could leave me and I would not be aware of it?"

"B-but . . . Papa said . . ."

"Your father is aboard the Turkish ship which will carry him to France," the Duke interrupted. "I have only one question to ask you, Zoia, and I wish you to answer me truthfully."

"What is . . . it?" she whispered.

"It is quite simple," the Duke answered. "I want you to tell me who you love best, your father or me."

For a moment she thought that she could not have heard him aright.

Then as she looked up at him, she had a fleeting glimpse of an expression on his face that she had never seen before, and she felt her heart turn over in her breast.

"It is a very important question," the Duke said, "because the choice is yours. I can take you now to your father so that you can leave with him, or you can stay with me."

It was impossible for Zoia to speak, and he went on:

"It is just a question of love; that is the answer I want you to give me."

"I . . . love you!" Zoia said. "I love you . . . desperately . . . but . . ."

The Duke's arms went round her, interrupting her.

"There are no 'buts,' " he said. "If you love me, if you really love me, that is all I want to know."

"I love . . . you!" Zoia said.

The words seemed to come from her very soul.

The Duke's arms tightened round her and as she lifted her face his lips came down on hers.

For a moment she was so bewildered by what had happened that she could feel nothing save amazement. Then the pressure of the Duke's mouth evoked the ecstasy she had always felt when they were close to each other, but now it was far more intense, more perfect, so that she wished she might die, because nothing could ever be so divine, so utterly and completely perfect.

His arms held her closer and his kiss became more demanding, more insistent, and she felt as if the fire that had burnt within her rose until it reached her lips and both she and the Duke were lost in the burning wonder of it.

How long the kiss lasted she had no idea. She only knew that when the Duke raised his head, words like music came from her in a paean of wonder.

"I love you . . . I love . . . you!"

"And I love you!" the Duke said. "I have loved you, my darling, ever since I first saw you. But I wanted to be well before I could tell you the depth and wonder of my love."

"C-can this be . . . true?" she asked. "Do you really . . . love me? I cannot believe it!"

"I love you! Now that you have made your choice, we are going straight away to be married."

"To be . . . married?" Zoia stammered.

"It will make things so much easier, my darling, when we set off for England, and I should tell you that I have already had your father's blessing."

"Papa . . . knows you intended to . . . do this?"

"When I knew that you were leaving me," the Duke said, "I was determined not to let you go."

"How . . . did you . . . know . . . I was . . . leaving?"

"You told me"

"I . . . told you?"

He smiled as his lips sought hers.

For a moment neither of them could speak. Then he said:

"It would be very difficult, my precious, for you ever to deceive me. When I watched you at dinner I knew what you were thinking, and when we sat together on the terrace I was sure of what had been planned."

"How...could you have...known that?" Zoia asked.

"Can you, of all people, ask that question?" he enquired.

She gave a little laugh, remembering how he had read her thoughts when she had first played to him.

"I then realised," the Duke went on, "that I had been somewhat remiss in not having taken action before. I found your father and told him what I wanted, and he agreed that as far as he was concerned it was a perfect solution to everything which had worried him."

"And Papa still...wishes to go to...France?" Zoia asked.

"He thought it was an opportunity not to be missed. Finding a neutral ship is not easy," the Duke replied, "and I think too he is being tactful, knowing that we would want to be alone together."

There was just a touch of anxiety in his voice as he asked:

"You do want to be alone with me, my darling?"

He knew her answer before the words came to her lips, and once again he was kissing her and, Zoia thought, drawing her very heart from her body and making it his.

The carriage came to a standstill.

"Everything has been arranged for us by one of His Excellency's very able Aides-de-Camp," the Duke said. "I thought, my precious, that you would like to be married in the faith to which your mother belonged. And it seemed appropriate when we are here in Russia."

"You...know it would...make me happy," Zoia said in a low voice.

The door of the carriage was opened and she saw that they stood outside a small Church. It was built in the ancient Russian style, painted with bright colours and with gold cupolas rising one above another.

The Duke took her hand and she was glad that she had a train to trail behind her as they moved into the Church.

There was the scent of incense, and there were hundreds of glittering lights before the sacred ikons which hung on every wall and every pillar.

A Priest was waiting for them, with two servers holding the Imperial Crowns which would be raised over their heads as they were married.

Zoia slipped her hand into the Duke's.

They were so closely attuned that she knew that for him the Service would be as sacred and binding as it was for her.

She was sure that her mother was close to her and inexpressibly happy that her daughter, like herself, had found the man she really loved.

"Thank you, thank you, God," Zoia prayed in her heart. "You have given me the man I adore. Help me to make him happy, and show me how to keep his love forever."

* * *

Driving away from the Church, Zoia felt as if she were in a dream and it could not really be true that she had passed through such a mystical, spiritual experience and still be in the ordinary, mundane world.

The Duke's arms were round her, and his lips seeking hers added to the illusion that nothing was real except him and their love.

He kissed her until she felt as if they were no longer human but Divine, and even closer still to God than they had been during the Wedding Service.

"My own perfect, lovely little wife," he murmured.

"Say that . . . again," she pleaded. "I was so certain so . . . convinced . . . that you could never marry me that I cannot . . . believe I am . . . really yours. . . .

"I will make you very sure of it in a little while," the Duke replied.

"You will . . . never . . . regret having , . . married me?"

"Only if you cease to love me."

"I shall love you completely every hour I live, with every breath I breathe," Zoia said passionately.

"My precious!"

The Duke's lips were on hers and she felt the passion draw a response from hers.

He kissed her until she felt breathless and her heart was beating wildly in her breast.

As the horses slowed down and the carriage came to a standstill, Zoia felt regretfully that they must come back to earth.

She supposed that the Governor-General and the *Duchesse* would be waiting to congratulate them on being married, but she shrank from the thought of anyone at this moment breaking in upon the intimacy and the closeness she felt in the Duke's arms.

Then as the door of the carriage was opened she realised that they were not outside the Palace but a much smaller building, also built of white stone.

She was suddenly aware that it was one of the small Pavilions that she knew were built in the grounds of the Governor-General's Palace and which she had been told were usually occupied by distinguished guests who brought their own retinue of servants with them.

The Duke once again knew what she was thinking, and he said:

"We shall be alone, my darling. I want it as much if not more than you do."

He drew her inside the Pavilion and shut the door behind them and she heard the carriage draw away.

Now there were flowers which scented the air and there were shaded lights to reveal that the place was furnished with many treasures, but there appeared to be no-one in the Pavilion but themselves.

The Duke drew her through a Sitting-Room, then beyond to a room lighted only by a few candles but in which was a magnificent bed hung with turquoise-blue silk from a corola of carved angels.

The ceiling was painted with gods, goddesses, and cupids, and on one wall there was a huge window from which the curtains were drawn back so that Zoia could see the stars.

With his arms round her, the Duke took her across the room to it and she realised that below them was the sea, reflecting the light of the pale moon so that it shimmered silver on the surface.

"This . . . cannot really be . . . happening!" she whispered in a low voice.

"It is happening, my darling," he replied, "and now at last you are mine! Not just for tonight but for all the years ahead, and beyond them for eternity!"

He pulled her close to him and went on:

"I believe that I have been searching for you through centuries of time, and now that I have found you, I will never lose you again."

"How . . . could you . . . say anything so . . . wonderful?" she asked. "It is . . . what I . . . too believe in my heart . . . but I thought I had to . . . go away."

"How could you imagine anything could matter except our love?" he asked. "How could you think for one moment that anything else was of any consequence?"

Zoia gave a little sigh and put her cheek against his shoulder.

"I thought you were part of the Imperial Splendour that I had seen in St. Petersburg," she said, "and which condemned my mother when she ran away from it."

"The only splendour that matters to us," the Duke said, "is the splendour of love—our love, darling— and I want you to tell me that you believe that is the truth."

"I have . . . always believed it," Zoia said, "but I thought, because you were so . . . important, because in the eyes of the Russians, Papa was presumptuous to marry Mama, you would never think me . . . good enough to be your . . . wife."

"You are not only my wife, but a spiritual ideal which I shall worship for the rest of my life," the Duke said.

"Suppose . . . I fail you?"

"I would stake the life you have given me that that will never happen!"

The note of sincerity in his voice made Zoia give a little cry and lift her face to his.

She thought he would kiss her. Instead, he looked down for a long moment into her eyes, and she knew that he was searching deep into her heart and finding what he had always sought.

He drew her away from the window and very gently took the diamond wreath from her hair and undid the train from her shoulders.

As it fell to the ground she trembled and felt shy as she felt his hands undoing her gown.

Then his lips held her captive.

The flames that Zoia felt deep within her rose higher and higher as he kissed her eyes, her lips, the softness of her neck, and her breasts.

She knew that the Duke was right and there was no splendour like their love.

What they felt for each other was part of the stars in the sky which glittered more dazzlingly than any jewels and deeper than the sea which moved beneath them.

The pomp and circumstance and the social distinctions which meant so much to those of Imperial rank were of no consequence.

"I love . . . you . . ."

The words seemed to vibrate between them, and the Duke answered:

"I love your beauty, my lovely wife, and adore your mind, but I worship your spirit and your soul, which speak to me in your music."

"I . . . told you . . . of my love?"

"I understood exactly what you were feeling, but tell me now that you love me and want me as I want you."

"I . . . want . . . you . . . I want you desperately . . . wildly . . . with all . . . of me."

"My precious, my adorable, mystical little wife!"

Zoia could feel the Duke's heart beating frantically against hers as he picked her up in his arms and laid her on the bed.

A moment later he was beside her, his lips seeking hers and his hands touching her body.

Then there was only him, and the fires that burnt within them burst into a conflagration.

The splendour of love covered them like the moonlight on the sea, and the ecstasy in their hearts carried them towards the stars, higher and higher until they became one and indivisible with the Divine.

ABOUT THE AUTHOR

BARBARA CARTLAND, the world's most famous romantic novelist, who is also an historian, playwright, lec-
turer, political speaker and television personality, has
now written over 250 books.

She had also had many historical works published
and has written four autobiographies as well as the
biographies of her mother and that of her brother,
Ronald Cartland, who was the first Member of Parlia-
ment to be killed in the last war. This book has a
preface by Sir Winston Churchill.

She had also recently completed a very unusual
book called "Barbara Cartland's Book of Useless Information," with a foreword by Admiral of the Fleet,
The Earl Mountbatten of Burma. This is being sold
for the United World Colleges of which he is President.

Barbara Cartland has to date sold 100 million books
over the world. She has broken the world record in the
last three years writing twenty, twenty-one, and twenty-
four books up to 1977. In 1978 she wrote twenty
books and sang an Album of Love Songs with the
Royal Philharmonic Orchestra.

In private life Barbara Cartland, who is a Dame of
the Order of St. John of Jerusalem has fought for

better conditions and salaries for midwives and nurses. As President of the Royal College of Midwives (Hertfordshire Branch) she has been invested with the first Badge of Office ever given in Great Britain, which was subscribed to by the Midwives themselves.

She has also championed the cause for old people, had the law altered regarding gypsies, and founded the first Romany Gypsy Camp in the world.

Barbara Cartland is deeply interested in Vitamin Therapy and is President of the British National Association for Health.